ZOEY DEAN'S
ALMOST FAMOUS

Zoey Dean's
Almost Famous

A TALENT NOVEL

Almost Famous

RAZORBILL

Published by the Penguin Group
Penguin Young Readers Group
345 Hudson Street, New York, New York 10014, U.S.A
Penguin Group (USA) Inc., 375 Hudson Street, New York, New York 10014, U.S.A
Penguin Group (Canada), 90 Eglinton Avenue East, Suite 700, Toronto, Ontario, Canada M4P 2Y3 (a division of Pearson Penguin Canada Inc.)
Penguin Books Ltd, 80 Strand, London WC2R 0RL, England
Penguin Ireland, 25 St Stephen's Green, Dublin 2, Ireland (a division of Penguin Books Ltd)
Penguin Group (Australia), 250 Camberwell Road, Camberwell, Victoria 3124, Australia (a division of Pearson Australia Group Pty Ltd)
Penguin Books India Pvt Ltd, 11 Community Centre, Panchsheel Park, New Delhi–110 017, India
Penguin Group (NZ), Cnr Airborne and Rosedale Roads, Albany, Auckland 1310, New Zealand (a division of Pearson New Zealand Ltd)
Penguin Books (South Africa) (Pty) Ltd, 24 Sturdee Avenue, Rosebank, Johannesburg 2196, South Africa

Penguin Books Ltd, Registered Offices: 80 Strand, London WC2R 0RL, England

10 9 8 7 6 5 4 3 2 1

Produced by Alloy Entertainment
151 West 26th Street
New York, NY 10001

Library of Congress Cataloging-in-Publication data is available

Printed in the United States of America

For Tom Shea

ZOEY DEAN'S
ALMOST FAMOUS

CHAPTER one

mac

◀ Sunday September 6 ▶

8 PM	Practice Le Strut for tomorrow
9 PM	Discuss social chair strategy w/ the Inner Circle
10 PM	Kate Somerville clay masks for all (skin must glisten on first day!)
10:30 PM	Beauty sleep

Get ready for B.Y.E.—Best Year Ever!

"Ladies, focus!" Mackenzie Little-Armstrong bellowed to her best friends, Evangelina Becks, Coco Kingsley, and, the newest member of their group, Emily Mungler. She clapped her Essie-polished hands together, her signature wooden bangles clacking on her wrists, and flipped her waist-length blond mane. "Ems needs to get this."

"This" was Le Strut, which was to be their grand entrance on the first day of eighth grade at Bel-Air Middle School, aka BAMS. Le Strut meant walking like you were too bored to care and therefore cooler than everyone who'd missed the memo on not caring. Hence the need to rehearse Le Strut nineteen times, with the video camera on Mac's white iBook providing instant playback for full analysis.

"Emily, you need to get into character," Mac said, her turquoise eyes focused on her computer screen. "Tomorrow is your debut as Cool New Girl at Bel-Air Middle

School, and right now you look like a sweet girl from Iowa who can't believe her luck."

"But that's exactly how I feel!" Emily protested, twirling a lock of her wavy, cinnamon brown hair.

Mac shook her head at the naïve Iowa transplant. She'd discovered the gap-toothed beauty faking her way into a premiere party and had instantly gotten a talent-crush on the girl's acting skills and *je ne sais quoi* adorableness. Just that morning Mac and her mother, the biggest talent agent in Hollywood, had convinced Emily to move to Bel-Air and pursue an acting career while she stayed in the Armstrongs' guest bedroom. Mac knew her starlet-in-training had it in her; it was *her* job to coax it out. "Get it right."

Emily nodded, closed her eyes, and inhaled deeply. She looked like she was doing yoga standing up, but Mac knew that was how Emily got into her acting zone. Then Emily opened her eyes and curled her lips into a half smile. She strutted confidently across the wooden floor, like a totally different person from the girl who'd tried the exact same thing only seconds ago.

They were in Coco's private dance studio, surrounded by wall-to-wall mirrors, for their annual night-before sleepover, which Coco, Mac, and Becks had enjoyed every year since first grade. Coco's father was the hotel mogul Charles Kingsley, and she lived in the top-floor suite of his King Bel-Air Hotel, which was a sprawling hacienda tucked off Stone Canyon Road.

Even though Mac, Becks, and Coco had discovered

their personal Le Strut years ago, it was always smart to fine-tune. Mac had insisted they rehearse in Coco's studio to get "the most honest" impression of what they really looked like. Mirrors, like iBooks, could lie, but mirrors + iBooks + Coco's high-tech studio = brutal honesty.

Mac hovered in front of her iBook like a football coach. "Good news," she said, her eyes narrowing. "We've got it!" She flipped the screen toward her friends so they could observe the playback of their work.

The iBook was divided into a split screen, each quarter playing a clip of one of the four girls striding across the dance studio. Emily's normally shy, hunched-over posture had improved tenfold (Mac had made her walk with a stack of French *Vogue*s on her head); Coco looked like a gazelle—dancing gave her excellent carriage—and even Becks's swagger was a little less tomboyish than usual. Mac strode confidently, her blond head held high.

"Le Strut is *parfait*!"

The girls smiled proudly.

"Okay, next order of business," Mac commanded, pulling up a new window on her iBook. She needed to strategize her upcoming campaign to win social chair, the holy grail of BAMS positions and also Mac's raison d'être. Voting was in three days, and Mac needed to make a splash with her campaign poster, which so far was a movie trailer poster of herself with the rating A for "Amazing."

"Now, I need your honest opinions. Is it too—" Mac was cut off by the ping of Coco's intercom.

"Pinkberry!" Becks bolted out of Coco's dance studio. Coco's French bulldog, Madonna, who had been asleep in her custom-made Louis Vuitton dog bed, yelped and chased after Becks.

Mac sauntered behind, Centurion AmEx in one hand and her iBook in the other, and Emily followed, smiling.

When Coco opened the door to the penthouse's private entrance, everyone gasped. The girl delivering their frozen yogurts was a total freakasaurus: She had buckteeth and long stringy hair dyed mauve, and there were plastic *Battlestar Galactica* pins all over her neon yellow vest. It was like she'd stepped off the pages of the *What Not to Wear, Ever* manual.

"Hi," Mac said finally.

"Hey!" Freakasaurus said, clutching the Pinkberry bag. She stood pigeon-toed and stared at Mac, then Emily, then Becks . . . and then, spotting Coco, her jaw dropped.

She pointed at Coco. "OH MY GOD, YOU'RE CARDAMMON'S DAUGHTER?!" The Pinkberry bag in her hand started to shake vigorously.

It was an unspoken rule in Hollywood that you didn't acknowledge fame. And rule number one was that you never, ever pointed at celebrities.

Mac shot a glance at Coco, who was hiding behind Becks. Coco was always a little touchy about the Cardammon subject. She was a pop-star-in-training herself and always worried she'd never measure up to her superstar mother.

"Are you okay?" Mac asked the Pinkberry freak. It was not a question; it was a polite way of saying, *Please stop spazzing out right now.*

"I've been in loooove with your mom since I was thirteen," the girl said, stretching her arms toward Coco like an opera singer. A tear trickled down her pasty cheek. "'Forever Blue,' like, got me through two breakups," she said, referring to one of Cardammon's eleven hit singles from the late '90s. "When I was—"

"That'sgreatthankshowmuchdoweoweyou?" Mac interrupted.

"Oh. Sorry." The girl handed Mac a receipt. Le Freak was still staring at Coco, mesmerized, like she'd seen a talking gnome.

"All righty, then." Mac signed the receipt briskly. "'Bye, now," she whispered. When the door closed, Mac waved her index finger around her ear to make the crazy sign.

"I've been in loooove with your mom since I was thirteen."

Mac spun around, wondering how Freakberry had gotten back inside the penthouse. Then she blinked. Twice. It was Emily. Her impression was so spot-on that for a second Mac had thought the girl was still there.

"'Forever Blue,' like, got me through two breakups," Emily continued. Then she pointed at Coco, her hand shaking, a real tear trickling down her cheek. "Oh my God—are you Cardammon's daughter?"

"Dude, you're freaking me out! It's too much like her!" Becks gasped, ripping into the paper bag and taking out two large frozen yogurts in white-and-green containers.

"Thatwasahmazing!" Coco agreed, taking her green tea–flavored fro-yo.

"You should see her be a guy," Mac said proudly, turning her clear plastic spoon upside down to lick the yogurt. "When Emily plays Jeff, she's so hot that girls have crushes on her. I mean, crushes on *Jeff*."

Emily covered her face, embarrassed. Earlier in the week, Mac had been trying to land Emily a role in a major Hollywood movie, *Deal With It*. The part was that of a girl who pretended to be a guy at boarding school. Mac had taken her budding star to the Grove, one of L.A.'s best shopping malls, and Emily had even fooled the Abercrombie salesgirl into thinking she was a guy. She'd also fooled Kimmie Tachman, BAMS's biggest gossip, whom they'd run into on their way out.

Mac set her iBook on Coco's antique writing desk and plopped into a wooden chair while Coco darted into her bathroom to scrounge through her Essie nail polish set. Emily sat cross-legged on the forest green carpet and started braiding her hair, and Becks flopped onto her back.

Mac reopened her computer, ready to revive the discussion of her campaign posters. Her home page was the Bel-Air community web page—a special, password-protected web community just for people in the 90077. Which was where she saw The Ad. Mac was stunned speechless for about two seconds.

"Oh my," she said suddenly, staring at the computer screen. The other girls rushed to Mac's side and read over her shoulder.

Seeking Personal Assistant

Very important Bel-Air social chair seeks assistant to provide daily support and help orchestrate big school fund-raiser. Must be organized, highly efficient, proactive, with great interpersonal skills, keen attention to detail, and a "can-do" spirit. Personal style is a plus, but not a requirement. Interested candidates: iChat RG here.

"It's just an ad." Becks crawled back to the carpet and went back to flipping through Coco's dog-eared *In Style*.

"Yes, but it's to work for *Ruby Goldman*!" Coco translated, shaking the bottle of cotton candy pink nail polish she'd chosen.

"Cha-ching!" Mac declared. Ruby Goldman was her biggest rival in the upcoming social chair elections. Ruby had spent the past four years trying desperately to steal Mac's style—she followed Mac's outfit choices like the North Star—and now here she was, already *hiring* for Mac's job.

"How can you tell it's Ruby?" Emily asked, brushing her hazelnut bangs out of her eyes.

"Social chair. Big school fund-raiser. Her initials: RG. Plus, *who else* would think this was a good idea?" Coco sat down on the carpet and started painting the nails on her left hand.

"Well, there's one way we can be sure." Mac grinned wolfishly at Emily.

"Don't look at me!" Emily shrieked. "I'm too new to make enemies!"

"Not *you*." Mac made air quotes. "Jeff."

"Jeff! Jeff!" Coco and Becks chanted.

Emily's eyes darted nervously around the room. She eyed Coco's bed as if she were thinking about darting underneath it.

"Oh, puh-leeeez!" Coco cried. "You have to!"

"Do it for the Inner Circle!" Becks said.

"Okay, fine," Emily groaned. "But I have a bad feeling about this."

Mac ran to her Hervé Chapelier overnight bag in the corner of Coco's room and promptly returned with a Stanford baseball cap that smelled like BO. Emily had worn Mac's brother's hat during her audition, and it had helped make her feel . . . masculine.

"Ladies, this is going to be fantastic," Mac said, licking her clear plastic spoon. "But Emily, Kimmie's probably told Ruby about 'Jeff' by now, so it's better to use another alias."

"Got it." Emily nodded. She plopped herself in front of Mac's white iBook and stretched her fingers like a pianist. She shook her head back and forth and rolled her shoulders in circles. She jutted her chin out from under her baseball cap. Then she cleared her throat to lower her voice a register. Watching Emily made Mac proud that she had a professional actress pulling the prank. Everything Mac did was A-list.

"Okay, everyone please move," Mac said, waving to the air around Emily. "Or you'll be in her interview."

Emily clicked on the link to video chat Ruby through the Bel-Air intranet. Coco, Becks, and Mac lay on the green carpet in a semicircle around Emily, hands on their chins so they could peer up at the computer screen.

"Hello, this is Ruby," said the voice. In the window on the laptop screen popped Ruby Goldman. Her long blond hair had newly fringed, sideswept bangs, and she wore high-waisted jeans and a red sleeveless blouse with ruffles, like she was in costume as a '70s movie star.

"Hey, I'm, uh, Tom," Emily said, her voice husky, her shoulders slouched. "I'm interested in the job."

Coco and Becks exchanged awed looks. Mac smiled.

"Are you new to Bel-Air, Tom? I thought I knew everyone. . . ." Normally Ruby talked in a fake baby voice, but now she sounded super grown-up.

"Yeah, my dad just got transferred here," Emily improvised.

"Great. Hi. I'm Ruby," she said, relaxing just a bit.

Coco dropped her clear spoon into her melting yogurt and leaned closer to the computer. Mac and Becks cupped their mouths to prevent their laughter from escaping.

"I'm about to be elected to a *very important* job at a *very important* school in Los Angeles," Ruby said. "It's too much for one person. And unfortunately, I can't clone myself." She sighed dramatically, as though it were a travesty that there was only one of her.

Becks reached for Coco's Hello Kitty notepad and wrote frantically with a purple gel roller: *Is she for reals?*

Mac shrugged. It didn't matter. They had stumbled upon the best entertainment ever in the history of night-before sleepovers.

"Wow, you sound really busy," Emily-as-Tom said in her deep, boy voice.

"I am. That's exactly it," Ruby said, fluffing her long blond hair and straightening the ruffle on her shirt. "But enough about me. Tell me about you. Why does a cute guy want to work for *me*?"

Mac's eyebrows shot up. Was Ruby *flirting* with Tom? Ew!

"I just thought the job sounded cool 'cause I'm organized and I like parties." Emily pulled her hat lower so that it covered more of her face.

Ruby crossed her arms. "Well, Tom, there are lots of *parties*, but I'm planning high-end events. *Grandes fêtes*. And I need someone who is hungry to learn. This job is the fast track to Bel-Air's best people."

"Yeah, I guess that's what I meant." Emily shrugged her shoulders.

"Listen," Ruby said, leaning in like she was about to tell a secret. "Let's interface and see if this would be a good fit. What's your e-mail address? I'll send you a confirmation."

"It's, uh, Tom, T-o-m. At e-m-a-i-l dot com."

"Great. I have a good feeling about this, Tom," Ruby said, nodding seriously.

Mac played with her wooden bangles, wondering how Ruby could be so stupid. The number one rule of the Internet was, never trust anything or anyone you meet online. Clueless people were always getting themselves into trouble with technology.

"Yeah, me too. Okay, see ya," Emily said, waving goodbye to Ruby.

The girls were quiet for several seconds before they erupted into laughter.

"*Grandes fêtes*!" Coco hyperventilated. "I can't believe she fell for it!" She looked at Emily seriously. "That was even better than your Freakberry impression!"

"Wait, wait, wait! Emily, puh-leeeez do more impressions!" Becks cried.

"Well . . ." Emily pulled the arms of her sweatshirt way down so it looked like she had no hands. Then she stood with her hand on her right hip, her left leg jutting out. "Totes!" she said.

"BECKS!" Coco and Mac screamed in unison.

"That *is* me!" Becks exclaimed, lifting up her sweatshirt arms to reveal that she'd tucked her hands inside. "Do more!"

Emily leaned her head down, getting into character. Then she popped her head up and tucked her hair behind her ears. She mimed twirling bangles on her wrists and checking her iPhone. Then she flipped her hair behind her back in one brisk motion and stared intently at her friends. She spoke in a slightly deeper, more business-like voice. "Girls, I have a plan!"

Mac blushed. Coco and Becks laughed. "Mac!"

"Don't do me!" Coco crossed her arms and shook her head in tiny, rapid back-and-forth motions. "I'll be too embarrassed!"

Emily crossed her arms and stared right at Coco. "Okay. I won't do you." She shook her head in the same tiny, rapid back-and-forth motions.

Coco covered her face in mock embarrassment.

"I have others," Emily said. She slowly curled her hand into a paw and made cat sounds. "*Meow!* Thanks for coming to my par-tay."

"*Kimmie Tachman!*" Becks and Coco cried. The girls had been to Kimmie's Sweet Thirteen party earlier that week. She had dressed as a sexy lion and had gone around making cat noises all night.

"That's exactly how she does it!" Coco cried. "It's sort of adorable, actually."

Becks, Coco, and Mac all started making paws and lion noises.

"Stop!" Coco puffed out her cheeks like a blowfish, then let out the air. She crossed her legs, twisting her ankles and pointing her toes. She looked like she was about to explode—her face was bright red and tiny beads of sweat glistened on her forehead.

"Meow!" Emily said again, making a paw.

"No, seriously, people, stop!" Coco spoke through clenched teeth. She was squeezing her fists tightly and her eyes were closed. "I'm serious!" Her breaths came in short pants, like Madonna's.

And then Mac realized—

"Oh, Coco," Mac said calmly, knowing that she had to call out the obvious. "Please tell me you did not just pee yourself!"

Coco turned an even brighter shade of red.

"Ew!" Becks yelled, cracking up even more.

"Just a drop!" Coco pleaded. "Nothing anyone would actually notice but me."

"And me, apparently," Mac pointed out.

"Okay, fine," Coco said, blushing. "When I laugh really, really hard, sometimes a little just comes out. I can't help it. Last year it happened at dance practice."

"Gross!" Mac said, and threw a green silk pillow at her friend.

"I know!" Coco laughed and threw a pillow back. "I'm gross! Can we please talk about someone else now?!" she said, shuffling into the bathroom to turbo-change.

"I have a secret." Becks said, jumping to her friend's rescue. She sat on her knees on the green carpet and the girls turned to face her. "It doesn't leave this room," she said slowly, and everyone nodded. She waited a few seconds, relishing the attention. "I've never kissed a boy."

Coco rejoined the circle and everyone groaned. None of them had kissed boys. Besides, the only datable boys at BAMS were Lukas Gregory and Hunter Crowe. They were best friends and water polo players, with really good fashion sense (Diesel jeans and plain tees) without being gay about it. All the other boys at BAMS were either (a) jerks, (b) immature, or (c) all of the above.

"That's right, these lips have never touched a boy," Becks went on, pointing to her naturally Angelina Jolie–esque pout. "But until they do, I have my ways. And that's what you *really* can't tell anyone."

Very slowly, Becks reached for her Pinkberry yogurt. "Pretend this is Austin," she said, referring to her next-door neighbor and crush. They'd grown up together, and this year he was starting at Bel-Air Prep. Becks drew the dessert close to her lips, and then she slowly opened her mouth and proceeded to *slobber all over the frozen yogurt,* making a mess of her face as she moved her lips over the fro-yo dome. By the time Becks had finished displaying her talents, there was just a messy puddle of melted frozen yogurt.

"Oh God, are you trying to make me pee again?" Coco asked.

Emily smiled, but resisted teasing anyone or laughing too much at their expense. *Well played,* Mac thought approvingly of her young star.

"Come on, Mac, don't you have any secrets?" Becks asked, putting down her mangled fro-yo and lying on her side.

"Yeah, we always tell you everything!" Coco squealed.

"Well," Mac said casually, "even after I win social chair I'm still going to hang out with you girls all the time. I have no interest in hanging out with anyone else at BAMS." Mac shrugged as if she'd just revealed a deep, dark secret.

"DUH!" Coco screamed.

"BIIIIIIG SHOCKER! Tell us something we don't know!" Becks commanded. "I want truly confidential information!"

Emily, Coco, and Becks stared at Mac wide-eyed. "Sorry, chickadees, you know everything about me," Mac replied nonchalantly, twisting the strap on her blue Splendid pajama top.

"Fine," Becks sighed. "I give up. And I'm tired."

"Me too," Mac said, realizing she'd lost the chance to revive her social chair strategy talks. They flicked off the lights and crawled under their Italian linens in the guest beds that housekeeping had wheeled in earlier that day.

Mac closed her eyes, grateful that she'd managed to dodge the *what's your secret* question. There was nothing she hated more than feeling vulnerable. And there was no faster way to become social roadkill than to be an open book.

Mac was half awake, half asleep, listening to the gentle hum of Coco's sound machine and thinking about how if she could just get social chair, her life would *finally* be complete when . . . it happened.

Brrrrrt!

Mac Armstrong farted.

Mac's heartbeat instantly raced at triple speed. She prayed that everyone was still asleep.

"Mac, was that you?" Coco squealed, sitting up, the whites of her eyes visible even in the dark.

"Maaaaaaaaaaaaaac! How could such a large sound come out of such a teeny girl?" Becks hollered, tossing a silk pillow at Mac.

"Oh, Mac, it really does reek in here," Emily said softly.

Mac blushed when she heard Emily's voice. Surely Mama Armstrong had never farted in front of her hotshot clients. She waited until the giggles subsided and the last of the pillows had been flung. "Fine. I'm lactose intolerant."

"Aha!" Coco exclaimed. *"That's* why you always get soy lattes!"

"No more Pinkberry for you!" Becks decreed.

"I'm sure we can all sleep better knowing my systems are working," Mac said. "But I need my beauty rest." She slipped on her baby blue Bliss satin eye mask. "Good night!"

"It *was* a good night until you farted," Becks teased.

Mac sighed. But in the darkness, she smiled to herself. It was great to have good friends. Friends who had your back no matter what. This was going to be a great year. The Best Year Ever.

CHAPTER TWO

emily

◀ Monday September 7 ▶

6:35 AM Style hair per Xochi's instruction to look bed-head chic. Leave bangs alone

7:25 AM Leave for school

8 AM Homeroom with Mac

AT SOME POINT TODAY: Figure out where classes/lockers/lunchroom/my life at BAMS are!

Emily took one last sip of her Moroccan mint tea latte and set the barely touched drink in the cup holder of the Toyota Prius. Mac's mom's assistant, Erin, had picked up the Inner Circle from Coco's hotel and was driving them to school in the Armstrong family staff car. Mac sat up front, and Emily was squished into the backseat between Coco and Becks. There was a fresh copy of *Variety* for Mac and the *L.A. Weekly* for Coco, who read the arts section to stay on top of dance performances she wanted to attend.

The Prius sailed along Stone Canyon Road, past eucalyptus trees and colonial-style mansions, and houses with names like La Cigogne and Jolie-Vie. Erin's weird flute music was playing on the CD player, but Emily was (almost) used to it by now, and it was (almost) relaxing and spa-like. It would have been a very peaceful ride, except for the fact that Emily's stomach was thrashing, and she felt as nervous as the day she'd auditioned for a major Hollywood movie.

And then she realized: She *was* auditioning.

Today was her tryout for the part of New Girl at Bel-Air Middle School. And, as Emily put her hand on her leg to stop it from shaking, she realized just how badly she feared being cast as The Girl Who Clearly Doesn't Belong in Bel-Air. Or worse: The Snob, which was how she'd been cast in Iowa, because no one had understood that she was really just shy. Today was her fresh start, riding to school with the coolest girls in Los Angeles, and she didn't want to blow it.

She bit her lip and inhaled, thinking of how every year before this she'd walked to school with Paige, her best friend, stopping on the way for chocolate French crullers at Winky's Donuts. She barely registered the Prius passing Demi and Ashton's Lexus hybrid SUV, or that Erin was turning onto famous Mulholland Drive. Emily didn't even notice the crystal-clear view of the Valley below, or the tourists who had stopped along the side to take pictures on the legendary road.

She only looked up when she heard Mac announce, "Time to bounce!"

Erin pulled over in front of an iron gate, wide open to reveal a redbrick driveway lined by pebbled walk-ways. Erin could have just turned up the driveway, but Mac had already explained that she didn't want their first steps on campus as eighth-graders to be clunky exits from the Prius. She wanted their first steps to be Le Strut.

As Emily took in Bel-Air Middle School, she almost stopped breathing. BAMS didn't look like a school—it looked like a large Spanish palace, with blazing pink bougainvillea hanging from its white walls. There was a giant grassy courtyard in the center, lined on all sides by white archways. It was perched on an incline, shrouded by eucalyptus trees overlooking Bel-Air on one side and the Valley on the other.

"Wait till you check out the view from up there." Mac slipped on her Gucci aviators.

"Now, be nice to all the awkward girls!" Erin said cheerfully, blinking her catlike green eyes. Erin was twenty-seven, but something about her always made her seem like a dorky sixth-grader.

"Girls, do you have everything?" Mac turned to the backseat and looked them over.

"It's all good," Coco said confidently, undoing the top button on her sleeveless vest and grabbing the oversize Dolce & Gabbana zebra print satchel at her feet. Coco's style was sophisticated, with a dash of eccentric.

"Yeah." Becks yawned loudly, rubbing her eyes and picking up her orange and black North Face backpack, the one Mac was never able to wrangle away from her.

Emily bent down to retrieve her *real* red Gucci bag. On Emily's first day in L.A., she'd bought a knockoff on Hollywood Boulevard, but Mac owned the real version, and had insisted Emily take it to school with her—something about the knockoff's buckles being obvio-faux. Emily felt a flash of awe—not to mention fear—over carrying an accessory that cost more than her mother's car.

Emily closed the door of the Prius and saw that the Inner Circle were already walking toward BAMS. To anyone else they just looked like bored girls who'd rolled out of bed, grabbed their expensive bags, and gone to class. But Emily knew her friends worked hard to get that look—it was Le Strut in action. Mac was in front, holding her iPhone at arm's length and pretending to check her messages. Becks and Coco were walking arm in arm, laughing like they were going to a party. Which meant that Emily, still by the Prius . . . was all alone.

"Mac! *Wait up*!" Emily screamed, running on the pebbles toward her friend.

Mac paused in her tracks, clutching her purple Mulberry Mabel bag, but she didn't turn around.

But Emily didn't have time to worry about how uncool it was to scream in public or to chase after someone—she was too terrified of walking into school all alone and looking like a loner. Or worse.

"Sorry, I thought you were going in without me," Emily said, sliding into step next to Mac.

"I know you're nervous, but for your own sake, don't do it again," Mac hissed. "First impressions are *everything*. And early buzz on you is very good."

"How do I have *buzz*? It's the first day of school!" Emily stammered. Sure, people in Iowa snap-judged you all the time—that wasn't new to Emily—but at least they waited until school *started*.

"I've been posting about you on the BA intranet," Mac said. "Just little notes like how everyone is totally gonna heart you." Mac cleaned her aviator sunglasses on the inside of her C&C pastel pink tank.

"Thank you, I guess?" Emily was starting to wonder if she needed social training wheels.

"You have to control your own press," Mac explained. "Otherwise people just believe whatever they hear." She sighed. "I'm just trying to keep you L.A. cool."

Emily rolled her eyes. Mac always made a distinction between Los Angeles and the rest of the word, as though the bar of humanity had been slightly raised for the City of Angels.

As their feet crunched on the pebbles, Emily focused on her BFF bangle, which she had finally convinced Mac to let her wear, despite the fact that it was "*très* summer camp." She could feel her right leg shaking slightly, and she was extra glad Mac had insisted she wear Mella flip-flops instead of heels.

Just before they walked through the main archway and onto campus, Mac paused. "In Hollywood, whenever the talent begins a project, she gets a start gift from her agent." She reached over to Emily and handed her a silver chain. "This is yours."

Emily looked down and realized there was a silver ring on the end. Emily daintily examined the ring. It was engraved INNER CIRCLE on the inside.

"It's custom-made by Sydney Evan," Mac said matter-of-factly. Mac lifted up her own chain with a silver ring dangling from the end, to reveal that she had the same one. "We all have them. Inner Circle, ring, get it?"

"Mac, I don't know what to—"

"No worries, babe," Mac said, waving her away. The girls walked in silence to the end of the driveway, a hundred sets of curious eyes watching them. When they reached the white pavement of the campus, they stopped in front of a giant fountain of Neptune. Mac turned to Emily. "I hate to bail on you, but all the social chair candidates have to go register in the main office." She tapped her purse, where her social chair posters were poking out, rolled into long thin tubes like museum prints.

"I have to check in for dance team captain auditions," Coco added.

"Yeah, I'm supposed to go to the athletic office, to ask about surf team funding," Becks chimed in.

Emily desperately wanted to say, *Can't it wait?* but she knew it was waaay too soon to get all Velcro on her new friends.

Mac pointed to Emily with her iPhone. "Don't worry—I'll text you the 411 on what you need to know. See you in homeroom." With that, Mac, Becks, and Coco skipped off, leaving Emily clutching her Gucci bag, all alone.

Emily took a deep breath and picked up her new, Mac-gifted iPhone, pretending to check her messages. Not that she had any. Paige was definitely not allowed to bring a cell phone to school, which meant she would be incommunicado until 2:30 p.m. Central time. Emily sat by the Neptune statue, hoping she would blend in. She checked the weather in Bel-Air: 78 degrees.

From behind her Gucci glasses (also from the Mac Armstrong lending closet), Emily peered out at her new school, wondering if everyone she saw was judging her the way she was judging them.

She spotted Ruby, standing in a group of girls whom she recognized from Kimmie Tachman's Sweet Thirteen birthday party. They were all wearing tight jeans and flowy tunic tops, in a close circle around Ruby. Ruby looked like a pop star with her glamorous flatironed blond hair, tight jeans, sparkly white tank top, and orange Creamsicle tan. She was standing on a step in the center of the group, holding a cordless microphone, singing a fiery song, like she was channeling Gwen Stefani.

Wham BAMS
Thank you, ma'am
You made me who I am

You taught me what I know
Not just a school
BAMS, you rule!

The song was a little batty, but Ruby looked like she was having the time of her life. Girls were smiling and nodding as Ruby sang. Even guys (cute guys!) in jeans and Reef sandals were nodding along.

When Ruby finished, she put the microphone down and giggled to her friends, who were clapping enthusiastically. The cute surfer guys whooped.

"Thanks, guys," Ruby said, fake-humbly. "That's a track from my new album. It's dropping this fall, and it's a taste of what you'll hear at ExtravaBAMSa . . . if I get elected social chair." She winked playfully at the boys.

Emily watched Ruby in awe. She'd never heard someone debut a song from an upcoming album at school. Apparently, she had a lot to learn about Bel-Air. She surveyed the crowd, hoping she didn't stand out in her James jeans and red Shadow Stripe racerback tank, all alone.

Emily had wanted to wear a dress—her only L.A. outings with the Inner Circle had been to VIP parties, where everyone wore designer cocktail dresses—but Mac had insisted the smartest strategy was to dress down. Emily realized Mac was right (as usual). Before her was a sea of sandals and cotton. No one looked like they were trying to be stylish, and yet . . . everyone looked amazing.

How did anyone stand out?

These kids looked like they'd been plucked straight from the covers of various clothing catalogues. Everyone had a very specific look. There was the Abercrombie group—girls dressed in colorful tank tops and faded jeans—walking through the archway and onto campus. The Anthropologie girls followed, three friends all wearing super-girly dresses with lace *and* bows on their behinds. Next Emily noticed two Billabong guys who looked like models playing Hacky Sack on the sprawling grassy lawn. At the end of the lawn she saw a group of guys in American Apparel hoodies, purple skinny jeans, dyed black hair, and red plastic sunglasses. Boys in Iowa didn't dress like that. A girl in an Urban Outfitters sundress and red polka-dot Toms shoes relaxed on the other side of the fountain, lying on her back reading *The Alchemist,* holding it with her right hand while her left dangled to the ground.

Emily blew out her bangs, trying not to stare at any one person for too long. What if the school principal took one look at her and deemed her unfit for BAMS? *I'm sorry, Miss, ah, Mungler, but we have a cool-people-only policy. And you'll notice on page twenty-seven of your handbook, clause F, that we do not accept students who have spent a significant amount of time in the Midwest.*

Emily was standing there when a text came through from Mac.

DNT 4GET 2 GO 2 RM 201 @ 759.

Well, at least Mac was looking out for her, Emily thought. She checked her Swatch. It was 7:55 a.m. Four minutes of painful, everyone-wondering-who-is-that-new-girl solo time. She stared at her iPhone again, wondering at what point it would become totally obvious that she was just trying to look busy, when she noticed a Rolls-Royce Phantom with the vanity plate E TACH pulling into the driveway.

Even though Emily was brand-new, she could figure out whose car it was: Kimmie "the Tawker" Tachman's father, Elliot Tachman, was known in the trade magazines as E-Tach. He was the most powerful producer in Hollywood, a guaranteed hit maker, and the man everyone wanted to work with. According to Mac, he was also the reason his daughter held high social status instead of just being known as a pink-obsessed musical theater nerd.

The car door opened and Kimmie bounded out, wearing a pink message tee that said PURRRFECT with Joe's jeans. She skipped toward Emily like a puppy charging after a ball. A bright, energetic, pink puppy.

"Hey, girl!" Kimmie put her hands on her hips and faced Emily. She always seemed a little too excited to see people. "My dad wants to say hi to you," she announced.

Emily winced. Elliot Tachman was the producer of *Deal With It.* He had been at her audition—and then rejected her in favor of redheaded super-starlet Anastasia Caufield. It was extra embarrassing because during the audition, Emily had been forced to improvise, and she'd even *kissed* Davey Woodward, her star-crush. Her heartbeat quickened just thinking about it. But what could E-Tach possibly want with her now?

Emily scoured the school grounds for some way to escape this inevitably awkward meeting, and then realized . . . she didn't know where anything was. Before she could stammer, *Maybe some other time,* Elliot Tachman himself emerged from the black Phantom. With his bulky frame and wild, curly hair, he looked like the giant wolverine on his navy blue Michigan sweatshirt.

"Hello, Emily," Elliot said, smiling. "I hear we get to keep *you* in Los Angeles for a little while."

Emily nodded. She'd heard that word traveled fast in this town, but this was *reallyfast*. She'd only moved in with the Armstrongs twelve hours ago. She hadn't even slept there yet!

Around her, a crowd of BAMS students headed toward the entrance seemed to slow, as if impressed to see some random girl talking to the multiple-Oscar winner. Emily blushed. Strutting across the campus with the Inner Circle was one thing, but getting attention on her own felt weird.

"Glad to hear it." Elliot nodded. "You know, everyone

was so moved by your audition. We want to find a part for you no matter what. My office will call your agency, but I wanted to tell you myself. I do hope you'll consider working with me."

Emily looked around her, as if he'd started speaking to someone else. She felt her throat go dry. Her right leg began trembling, then her left leg. She felt weak and excited at the same time: Elliot Tachman had just offered her, Emily Skyler Mungler, a role. *In a Hollywood movie.*

"Thanks," Emily said calmly, but inside she was buzzing. She wished Mac were there to say the perfect thing, because Emily had no idea what you were supposed to say when the biggest producer in America offered you a job. "That sounds like fun."

"Great. We'll be in touch." Elliot waved. Then, looking right at Kimmie, he said, "And you. Behave. Or else." He made a "grrrrr" sound like a bear.

"Duh, Da-dee!" Kimmie said, giggling and making a bear paw back. Elliot disappeared into the Phantom, and it drove off immediately.

Turning to Emily, Kimmie cried, "I can't wait to tell *eh-ver-eee-one* your news!" Emily was still too stunned to say anything. "Are you in homeroom with me and Mac?" Kimmie asked slowly, as though she were talking to a small child.

Emily nodded weakly. Her brain had shut down.

"All righty, then. We should go," Kimmie said. Emily

was so excited she barely noticed Kimmie grabbing her hand and leading her to homeroom.

Emily took one last look at the BAMS grounds, smiling. What had she been so worried about before? She *belonged*. Not only that, she was going to be Bel-Air's newest starlet-in-residence.

CHAPTER THREE

COCO

◀ Monday September 7 ▶

7:55 AM Le Strut

12 PM Bam-Bams captain audtions!

Coco's heart skipped a beat as she opened the blue double doors to the BAMS auditorium. The stadium-style leather seats were packed. True to BAMS policy, the whole school was invited to the captain auditions for the Bam-Bams, the dance team. Anyone could walk in and watch.

Or snicker.

Coco was always a little afraid that kids would make fun of her behind her back because her mother was Cardammon—and she *wasn't*. Having a living legend for a mom made it difficult to feel accomplished.

She breathed a sigh of relief when she spotted Mac, Becks, and Emily sitting in the third row, two rows behind the Bam-Bams, taking pictures of themselves with their iPhones. Mac had brought bento boxes for them all for lunch. Becks looked up from a dragon roll to wave hello.

"You ready?" Mac whispered, turning her phone to snap a picture of Coco.

"I guess so." Coco shrugged and began her stretches in the area to the side of their seats. She took a deep breath to calm her nerves. This audition was about so much more than just *dancing*. Earlier that week, Coco had tried out for Brigham Powell, the most powerful music producer in the world—along with her Bam-Bams teammate Ruby Goldman. But Brigham had passed on Coco and had instead signed *Ruby* up for a record deal. Apparently, Coco needed more work. Unfortunately, today was Coco / Ruby showdown number two, as Ruby was up for captain as well. Ruby had always been an amazing dancer, but ever since she'd lost forty pounds over the summer, she'd had a sparkling confidence that gave her an extra edge. Coco was dreading the idea of losing to Ruby again, especially since she'd wanted to be captain for years. It was the ultimate leadership position, because the Bam-Bams didn't have a coach, just a "faculty advisor." The captain chose all the routines, scheduled the practices, and was even in charge of booking all the group's shows.

Coco took a sip of her citrus-flavored Vitamin Water just as she spotted Ruby entering the auditorium. One of Ruby's minions, Haylie Fowler, stood to her side with her arms crossed, more bodyguard than friend. Since Ruby had lost all that weight, Haylie was now the only truly fat girl in their grade. She was also an alternate on the dance team, but had never actually gotten to perform. Coco almost felt sorry for Haylie: Everyone knew that the only reason she was still on the team was because her father owned the Grove, the best outdoor shopping mall in L.A., and she hooked the team up with their prestigious holiday show every year. Haylie was untouchable.

Ruby was dressed in stretchy gold lamé pants and a black T-shirt that hung off one shoulder and exposed her shiny gold sports bra. Her yellow-blond hair was teased in a side pony. She looked like she was an extra in the 1980s movie *Flashdance.* Mac jabbed Coco in the ribs, making sure she'd seen Ruby's outfit choice. But the gold and black getup didn't make Coco scoff; instead she felt silly for having chosen so conservatively—she was wearing black leggings and a black American Apparel tee. She looked like a nerdy grad student compared to her nemesis.

Ruby and Haylie walked slowly across the auditorium and squeezed themselves into the second row, right in front of the Inner Circle and right behind the dance team. Technically anyone could be on the team, even boys, but in reality the Bam-Bams was an exclusive club for some of the cutest, most connected girls at school.

Mac, Emily, and Becks stopped playing with their cell phones long enough to give Ruby and Haylie a *you're not welcome here* stare. If Ruby noticed, she didn't let on. She dropped her coffee-colored leather Club Monaco duffel on the floor and sat down to face the stage, her back to the Inner Circle.

Snippets of Ruby's conversation and her oh-so-annoying baby voice floated back to Coco. "And then I said to Brigs, 'I'm only thirteen, I can't drive!'" Haylie laughed like that was the funniest thing she'd ever heard in her entire life. "And then he asked me if I was *rehearsing* for dance captain auditions. And I was like, 'Um, hellooo, are you crazy?' That's, like, an insult to my level. Can you *imagine*?"

Coco looked down at the ground, hoping that none of her friends had heard Ruby's comment, because Coco had spent *hours* choreographing a dance to Rihanna's "Umbrella." She'd taped herself from every angle, changed the dance four times, and repeatedly asked her mother's opinion.

Ruby and Coco had each been given two days to devise a routine that, in theory, the dance team could perform. Coco desperately wanted to impress the younger members of the team, who voted on a captain based on choreography, dance skills, and of course the unspoken x-factor: popularity. But Coco also wanted to impress herself. She wanted to be proud of her dancing again. She'd been so depressed after her Brigham audition that she'd almost quit.

Coco pressed her Stila-glossed lips together, wishing the din of the noisy room were even louder so that she couldn't hear their voices. She was imagining how stupid she would feel when she did her very practiced, very coached dance, and then Ruby blew her away with something effortless. It was so unfair how some people were born with Talent, and Coco had to get by with Hard Work. She kicked her foot up on the chair in front of her—Ruby's seat—and tied the laces of her black jazz shoes a little tighter.

Ruby turned around, very slowly, when Coco's shoe tapped her chair. "Oh, hi, Coco! I didn't see you!" she said with fake surprise. "Hey, Mac, Becks, New Girl . . ."

"Hi," Coco replied evenly, slowly removing her foot from Ruby's chair. She could feel Mac tense beside her.

"I've been soooo busy with Brigs and career-planning, I haven't had time to check in. How *are* you?" Ruby asked fake-sweetly, teasing some blond hairs in her side pony.

"Fine," Coco said through gritted teeth.

"Ruby, why didn't you tell me it was Back to the '80s Day!" Mac jumped in, eyeing Ruby's ensemble. "I wish I'd known. I would have worn something . . . ugly."

Ruby laughed like this was a joke instead of an insult. A beat too late, Haylie followed along, letting out her screechy laugh. She sounded like a horse. Coco felt bad for Haylie, who, in addition to being large, was knock-kneed. Behind her back, people called her SSD (Seven-Second Delay) because she was so slow. "Oh, Macdaddy," Ruby sighed. "You're so funny."

"You know what's funny?" Mac replied instantly. "Your outfit."

"You know what's sad?" Ruby asked sweetly. "How you're gonna lose social chair." Her tone was so Splenda-sweet the words sounded like a compliment.

"Snore." Mac threw her arms up to fake-yawn, her wooden bracelets clunking. "Wake me up when Ruby stops talking." Emily and Becks giggled. More than anyone they'd ever met, Mac was *so* not afraid of confrontation. Maybe it came from having a no-nonsense agent mother.

"Don't sleep too long or you'll miss my social chair victory speech." Ruby flashed a coy, Paris Hilton smile.

Coco glared at Ruby, about to say something. And then she realized . . . *it was all a total waste of energy.* Instead, Coco decided to spend her energy on herself. She put on her Bose noise-canceling headphones and listened to the *Dreamgirls* sound track, tuning out everyone. She imagined performing the best she could. She mentally ran through her routine: double pirouette, barrel turn, hip walk, hip fall. She envisioned stretching her arms out vigorously, nailing her turns, and smiling all the way.

Coco had spent the summer training with the most revolutionary dance teacher in London (arguably the world)—Marcel Marcel, the man who had made her mother a pop star. He'd taught Coco to let go and "feel" the music. It had taken all summer, many failed moves, and much sharp-tongued criticism, but eventually his staccato commands had become fewer and fewer, until

Coco could dance his style without Marcel having to whisper a word.

Vivian Kelley, the school's athletic director, walked to the front of the stage. She had broad shoulders, and was shaped like a rectangle. Today she wore a navy blue tracksuit, her thick brown hair hanging down like drapes. She looked like a man wearing a wig. "All righty, everyone, let's get this party started," Vivian called out, clapping her meaty hands together. "As a reminder, we will be having a dance-off for the role of Bam-Bams captain, between two of the eighth-graders on the team: Ruby Goldman and Cordelia Kingsley."

The Inner Circle applauded furiously at the sound of Coco's name, and, in front of them, Haylie whooped for Ruby. The Bam-Bams in the front row remained quietly nonpartisan.

"One lucky girl will be chosen to choreograph the routines of the world famous Bam-Bams!" Vivian continued. "I'm going to call one of the names at random, and each of our dancers will perform a quick two-minute routine. Of course, you can all cheer, but only the Bam-Bams can vote." She eyed the front row, where the seven other members of the dance team were sitting holding ballots: the twins, Lucia and Maribel Peets; Alexa Harris, whose father owned Harris jeans; Eden Singer, whose mother, Anabelle, was a former reality TV star and supposedly cuckoo; and the sixth-graders—Anais Lindly, Taylor White, and Ames Evershod. They were all dressed in their black Lululemon workout pants with a hot pink waistband, because the clothing company had recently decided to sponsor the team in a bid to win over young tastemakers.

Onstage, Vivian was still talking. "I want you all to show your support for our amazing dancers and all the hard work they've put into the team for the past two years. It's gonna be off the hook!" She pulled a slip of paper out of her tracksuit pocket. "Cordelia, you're up first!" she announced, and man-walked off the stage.

Coco realized Mac was nudging her to go. She removed her headphones, dropped them into Mac's open palm, and walked confidently down to the stage.

Coco assumed her first position: head bent, arms behind her back. She'd decided not to use an actual umbrella, because that seemed too cheesy. But she was trying to invoke the idea with her arms. The opening beats of "Umbrella" began to play over the auditorium's powerful sound system, and Coco took two deep breaths, let out the air, and then went for it. She turned her leg in a half circle, leapt forward, and then actually landed her first double pirouette. Very easily. And the rest of the dance only got easier, even though the moves were technically more difficult. Her barrel turns felt as natural as walking. *I love dancing*, she remembered. She didn't think about Ruby, or her pop star mother, or the Inner Circle. She didn't look out at the other dance team members, wondering what they thought of her. She didn't even think about the crowd.

At the end of the dance, Coco pulled her foot in and spun around four times in a row. It was a turn she'd missed often in practice, but this time, she held on to the ending.

Coco's breaths slowed, and she let her focus return to BAMS. She looked out into the auditorium and saw rows of smiling—not snickering—faces. Coco beamed proudly and walked back to join her friends, who were jumping up and down as though she'd just won an Olympic gold medal.

Ruby was already taking the stage.

Coco didn't want to watch. She didn't want to have to feel inferior again, especially not after the high of the performance she'd just given. She decided to stretch by the side of the row of seats, deliberately facing the back of the auditorium instead of the front. Still, she couldn't help but overhear her friends.

"What in the world is Ruby *doing*?" Mac hissed.

"She looks like she's about to eat it," Becks said, a little too loudly.

"Oh, jeez. Did she even learn a dance?" Emily asked softly.

Coco turned around to peek at RG.

Ruby's moves were, as always, perfect, and she'd chosen a series of incredibly difficult spirals and fan kicks. But she hesitated after each move, as if unsure of what came next. Her face was contorted in a strained expression, rather than the exuberant smile they'd always been told to wear during a performance. Suddenly Coco realized: *She was trying too hard.* Coco held her breath as Ruby brought her arms in for what Coco instantly recognized was a difficult, five-rotation spin that even Cardammon in her heyday might have missed.

Ruby opened her arms mid-spin and careened to the wood-paneled floor of the stage with a thud.

"*Ow!*" she screeched. The music stopped. The auditorium filled with hushed whispers as two hundred curious people leaned toward the stage for a better look.

"My ankle!" Ruby leaned on her back, staring at her feet, which were crisscrossed. She seemed stuck in her own body.

Vivian Kelley ran over and tried to lift Ruby to her feet.

"Don't move me!" Ruby barked, as though Vivian were her assistant and not a school administrator. Coco automatically made her way to the stage, feeling like she should do something. She paused at the front row and watched in disbelief as Haylie escorted Ruby off the stage and out the auditorium's back doors, practically carrying her fireman style.

The dance team huddled together in a semicircle, while Coco stood on the floor in disbelief. When the girls broke apart from their circle, Lucia Peets, a very influential seventh-grader on the dance team, whispered to Coco from her seat. "You were *phenom*," she said. Lucia had icy blue eyes and long brown hair, and she and her twin sister, Maribel, were rumored to want to co-run for social chair next year.

"For reals," Maribel chimed in, her blue eyes sparkling. "We totally voted for you," she hissed confidentially as she handed a stash of dance team ballots to Vivian.

"Thanks," Coco said sheepishly.

Vivian walked back to the center of the stage, holding the ballots in her hand. "All right, everyone, now that Miss Goldman is, uh, finished with her performance, it's time for me to announce your new captain. I'm sure you're all eager to get back to class. NOT!" She chuckled at her own non-joke. "Well, I'll make this brief. The sixth- and seventh-graders have chosen a dance team captain. And that captain is . . ."

There was a pause. Coco looked around, wondering whatever had happened to Ruby, and whether the other team members would rely more on today's dance-off or on past performances to make their decision. What if they decided Ruby had performed better for the last two years? What if they felt bad for Ruby and voted for her out of pity? Coco curled her toes in her jazz flats to stay calm.

"Drumroll, please . . . Your new BAMS dance team captain is . . . *Cordelia Kingsley*."

Mac, Becks, and Emily stood up and cheered, and the rest of the school followed. Coco looked down at the floor, mildly embarrassed that the Inner Circle was shrieking so loudly—she heard Becks whoop like a guy, "YEAH, COCO!"—but mostly, she was proud that she had such great friends on her side. Mac held her iPhone up to take a photo. "Do a victory dance!" she cried out.

Coco grinned from ear to ear. She was maxed out on dancing for the moment. The thought of another pirouette was excruciating. Instead, she high-fived Becks and did a victory strut.

CHAPTER FOUR

becks

◀ Tuesday September 8 ▶

7:55 AM	Do the Le Strut thing
8 AM	School
2:59 PM	Out of school
3:36 PM	Surf, surf surf!!!

Becks dragged her favorite surfboard, her Al Merrick daisy-covered beauty, down to the deserted semiprivate beach behind her house. There were few things in the world that Becks loved more than surfing in the afternoon, when the Malibu air was hot and the ocean felt perfectly breezy by comparison. The early September sky couldn't have been bluer, and the waves were soft and slow.

Becks plopped her board onto the sand; she wanted to do some yoga poses before hitting the waves. Cat, cow, inhale, exhale. Just like she'd practiced with her father and their yoga guru, Vikram, every morning in Hawaii this summer. Becks had always thought yoga was ooky-spooky, but one day, after a lesson, she'd seen Vikram surf the North Shore in a series of fearless, loose lines, like he was weightless on his board. Becks had promptly rethought her stance.

From the downward dog position, she could see

Steven Spielberg's house in the distance. She inhaled and shifted her gaze to take in her own giant stucco house with its enormous glass windows. Becks's mother had died when she was a baby, and it had been just Becks and her dad, Clutch, living in that house for as long as she could remember. Her father had put her on a board when she was just three years old, meaning Becks had surfed before she'd learned to ride a bike. But that was natural for someone related to Clutch Becks, who had been the star of his own prank show, *That Was Clutch*. He'd made MTV so much money that they'd designed him a special house out of gratitude (and, of course, to use for reunion movies). While Clutch was retired now, his prank-show buddies still came over all the time, often attempting stunts that were both death- and logic-defying.

Becks took out her piña colada–scented surf wax and began waxing her board. Out of the corner of her eye, she spotted a familiar goldendoodle bounding toward her—*Boone*. And if Boone was nearby, that meant his owner, Austin Holloway, was not far behind. Austin was one year older than Becks and was starting freshman year at Bel-Air Preparatory School, aka BAPS. Becks scanned the sand and spotted her crush jogging toward her, holding a dog treat shaped like a cupcake.

Becks and Austin had grown up together, and for years she'd treated him like a brother. They gave each other wedgies and had veggie dog–eating contests

(Becks usually won). Their hangouts were always some version of surf / eat / make fun of each other.

Until last week. When Becks saw Austin for the first time after being apart all summer, something had changed between them. Now, every time she saw Austin, with his new arm muscles and longer hair, she wasn't sure how to behave around him. The one thing she *did* know was that she couldn't stand how discombobulated he made her feel. Like now, her body felt as wobbly as Jell-O, and her heart was fired up like the time she'd tried one of Mac's Red Bulls.

Austin's shaggy brown hair was flopping over his eyes and down his nose. He wore a long-sleeved Rusty tee that was now too tight in the sleeves, and cargo shorts with big pockets down the legs. He looked boyish but adorable—too adorable, actually. Becks wanted to hide.

"What happened to you the other day?" Austin asked, swatting Becks with his ratty blue towel as he reached her side. "You ditch me for the *ick*?" he teased, referring to his nickname for the Inner Circle. He pretended to throw up.

"Could you not talk about my friends that way?" Becks said, putting her hands on her hips defiantly, pretending to be annoyed. But inside she was buzzing at being so close to Austin, even if he was making retching noises.

"Dude, you just, like, took off. Why were you MIA?"

He stopped fake-vomiting and looked at her, patiently expecting an answer.

Becks pretended to be really focused on slathering her right arm with Coppertone SPF 45. The last time she'd seen Austin, he'd been flirting with big-boobed Ellie Parker, even carrying her board for her, as he taught her to surf on *their* beach. Ellie was one of Ruby's newest minions, a bubbly blonde with a tiny body everywhere except for her naturally big chest. Becks had bailed because watching Austin act stupid just to please some annoying girl made her heart ache.

She looked down at the sand, digging a hole with her right big toe. "I figured you two wanted to be alone."

"Me and Ellie?" Austin asked incredulously, running his fingers through his hair with both hands. He sounded so sincere that Becks actually dared to look up into his blue-gray eyes. He looked off at the ocean, as if he'd already forgotten the day and was trying to remember. "Nah . . . Ellie just wanted me to show her how to surf." Austin shrugged. "I'm always willing to teach a newbie."

"That was it?" Becks asked. Boone rubbed against her bare leg and she ruffled the shaggy fur on his golden head.

"Dude, Ellie can't surf. She can't even get on her board." He made a face that indicated he found not being good surfer as unattractive as having warts all over your body. A sunbeam landed on his messy hair, making him look even more golden. "You ding-dong! You know I couldn't hang with a girl who can't surf." He mussed Becks's hair, giving her noogies.

Becks knew from the heat in her cheeks that she was full-on blushing. She bent down to nuzzle her face into Boone's soft fur just to hide her rosy glow.

"Hey, I gotta meet with a surf coach tomorrow, but we should hang Wednesday," Austin said. "You around?" He swatted her again with his towel.

Becks felt a surge of excitement wash over her. *We. Should. Hang.* The greatest three words ever.

She counted to two in her head so that she didn't sound overeager, then stood slowly. *Pretend like you're talking to Mac. Pretend like you're talking to Mac.* Her heart was pounding. "Sure, I'm around."

"Great. *Hasta miércoles,*" Austin said, punching her in the shoulder.

"Yeah, see you Wednesday," Becks chimed back. She smiled into his eyes for a second, before realizing he was leaving without hopping in the water. "Wait. Aren't you going to surf?" Becks asked.

"Nah. I just came by to say hi." Austin grinned and took a few steps backward toward his house.

As she caught his blue-gray eyes with her gaze, all Becks could think was: She had a date. With Austin. It didn't get any better than this.

CHAPTER FIVE

mac

◀ Tuesday September 8 ▶

8 AM	Homeroom with Ems
12 PM	Lunch (how many days in a row is too much sushi?)
12:30 PM	Last-min. tanning, SPF 30
2:55 PM	School's out (T minus 17 hours to SC election!)

Mac walked down Main Hall en route to Mr. Anderson's homeroom. She was wearing the Inner Circle's campaign outfit: Hudson jeans and the *pièce de résistance:* the "Team Mac" T-shirt, designed expressly by Cardammon. It was a plain navy tee with a snug rocker fit that said TEAM MAC in all caps across the chest. It was simple, understated, and cool. Coco, Becks, and Emily had distributed the tees that morning in the BAMS driveway. Her hips swiveled as she stepped: She was working it. She smiled slyly when she realized that she had definitely been noticed by the two cutest boys at BAMS: Lukas Gregory and Hunter Crowe. They were standing under an archway checking their BlackBerries. Lukas had brown hair, dark eyes, and a chiseled face, and Hunter looked like a junior version of Matt Damon.

Mac's Jimmy Choo Mary Janes clicked as she walked down the red-tiled hall, her eyes deliberately hidden behind her Gucci aviators so no one could tell she was really performing a status check. What she noticed, in this order, was:

1. The Team Mac posters had *not* been tampered with.
2. Ruby's posters were MIA. (Were people pulling down Ruby's posters?)
3. Spotted: Six girls wearing Team Mac shirts. Just in Main Hall.

If Mac had not decided to stop smiling in public because pouting was way cooler, she would have cracked a *très* goofy grin right then.

"Good luck!" A brunette in a Team Mac tee came up to her. The girl had a sweet face and brown eyes. Mac tried to remember her name but drew a blank.

"Thanks," Mac said, blowing a Chanel lip-glossed kiss. "That means a lot." With a final nod of appreciation, she clicked down the hallway toward her locker.

Mac knew she sometimes got ahead of herself, and she couldn't get too excited about social chair, because she hadn't won. *At least not yet.*

The lockers at BAMS were bright red, had digital combinations, and were nearly four feet high, in case long coats came into style. Mac had petitioned for locker number 622, which spelled out M-A-C on the buttons of her iPhone. As she started to punch in the combination, she spotted a pink blur out of the corner of her eye.

It was Kimmie Tachman, wearing a pink Abercrombie hoodie with a Team Mac T-shirt underneath. She slunk over to Mac's locker and looked over both shoulders like a spy.

"Nice shirt," Mac noted, stunned that Kimmie was being so bold about supporting Mac. "Where's your boss?"

"Look, I can't hate on Ruby," Kimmie whispered. "I already invited her to come to Maui."

"So why are you talking to me?" Mac asked nonchalantly, checking her perfectly glossed pout in the compact she always stored in her locker. She kept triplicates of all her beauty products so she didn't have to worry about transferring from home to Prius to school.

"I thought you'd like to know—Ruby's ankle is broken with a capital *B*," Kimmie hissed, looking over her shoulder again. "Her deal with Brigham fell through! According to very informed sources, you're leading social chair polls ninety to ten."

Mac raised her right eyebrow. She wasn't sure if she should—or could—believe the Tawker. After all, Kimmie was publicly Team Ruby. Could it be a trick? Or could it be that Kimmie recognized power and wanted to give her allegiance where she knew it would soon be rewarded?

A conundrum.

But before Mac could say anything, Ruby appeared from around the corner, hobbling on a set of shiny silver crutches coated in glitter and faux diamonds. Mac fought the urge to gasp—Kimmie wasn't kidding. Ruby really *was* hurt. She stopped at her locker, which was just across the hall from Mac's. (Number 782—Ruby always copied Mac, and had petitioned for a locker that spelled out *her* name. But really it just spelled out RUB.) Haylie Fowler and Ellie Parker stood on either side of Ruby, holding her books.

Kimmie immediately took a step away from Mac and zipped up her hoodie, hiding her Team Mac T-shirt. She joined Ruby, Haylie, and Ellie as though her conversation with Mac had never happened.

"Ruby, I have your history textbook right here." Kimmie patted her oversize Coach bag, which she used as a backpack. But she looked back and smiled knowingly at Mac.

"Well, if it isn't the soon-to-be-loser of social chair," Ruby snickered, spotting Mac. Haylie proceeded to open Ruby's locker and carefully hang Ruby's white jacket inside.

Mac sized up the new group, who were so clearly trying to copy the Inner Circle. Ellie was wearing a miniskirt that showed her stick-thin legs, and even Haylie looked like she'd dropped a few pounds. "If it isn't the Thinner Circle!" Mac smirked, pleased at her new nickname for Ruby's group of newly skinny Inner Circle wannabes.

"I'll take that as a compliment," Ruby said, leaning on a shiny crutch.

"Yeah, thanks for the cohm-pliment," Haylie said, totally overdoing the friend backup.

Ruby shot Haylie a *shut up* glance and Haylie looked down at the ground nervously, chewing a cuticle.

"Um, can we hit pause for a second?" Mac said, eyeing the sparkles on Ruby's crutches. "Did you BeDazzle your crutches?" She said *BeDazzle* like you would say *barf all over.*

"They're titanium," Ruby snapped defensively, gripping the handles of her crutches a little tighter. "Engineered just for me by the designers at Porsche."

"That's very, um, reality show of you." Mac shrugged, snapping shut her compact. She was about to say, *Thanks for showing us why Porsche should stick to car design,* but then decided it wasn't any fun to kick someone when she was already so clearly down.

"So, Mackerel, I hear your friend made dance captain," Ruby said bitterly. Haylie and Ellie smiled smugly behind her, and Kimmie played with the zipper of her sweatshirt, as if unsure what to do. "At least this time she didn't freak out and make a fool of herself in front of a major record producer."

Mac slammed her locker shut and glared at Ruby. Disrespecting Mac was one thing. Disrespecting the

Inner Circle was another. "At least *she* didn't get a dance contract and then *blow it*. Have a good day!"

With that, Mac spun around on her Mary Janes and clicked down the hallway. Without looking back at Ruby and her minions, she threw a little skip into her step.

Just because she knew Ruby couldn't.

CHAPTER SIX

emily

◀ Wednesday September 9 ▶

6 AM	Wake up
6:35 AM	Give up on trying to style my hair per Xochi Dawn
7:05 AM	Breakfast at Polo Lounge (!)
7:55 AM	Le Strut (do we do this every day?)

AT SOME POINT TODAY: Still need to figure out where everything is!

2:55 PM	School's out
6:30 PM	iChat Paige (iChat is a pain)

Emily stared at her egg-white frittata, sliced pink grapefruit, and flourless toast, debating which would be the least messy to eat. Not that Adrienne Little-Armstrong or Mac would notice if Emily spilled on the pastel pink tablecloth.

They still hadn't even noticed Jake Gyllenhaal in a booth in the corner, tucked behind a copy of *Variety*. Maybe this was just a typical breakfast at the Polo Lounge, but Emily was not used to seeing A-list celebrities before school started, and she *really* wasn't used to taking power breakfasts with Hollywood's top talent agent, aka Mac's mom. Who, at that exact moment, was checking her BlackBerry with her right hand and stabbing her egg-white omelet with her left. Mac sat next to Emily taking notes on her iPhone and sipping her papaya-banana breakfast smoothie.

Emily decided the frittata was the safest choice, and

relaxed when it broke apart quite cleanly in a dainty, non-attention-grabbing bite.

"So how do you like BAMS so far?" Adrienne asked absentmindedly. She sounded like she was reading off an e-mail.

By the time Emily realized Adrienne was talking to her, it was too late. Adrienne had already moved on. Like her daughter, Adrienne had a charming / scary way of firing information at someone.

"She needs acting lessons. Let's call Larry Moss," Adrienne said, tapping Mac's phone with her polish-free fingernail. Mac nodded politely to show that she'd heard and tap-typed *Larry Moss* into her iPhone. Mac was being oddly, enthusiastically obedient at this meeting, Emily noticed. It was the Adrienne Effect—she made people behave. "Don't take it personally, Emily," Adrienne added. "Everyone in this town has a coach for everything."

"I'd love to meet Larry Moss," Emily said, not letting on that she knew he'd worked with Leonardo DiCaprio *and* Hilary Swank *and* Helen Hunt. All Emily wanted was to avoid saying anything that would remind Adrienne that she had way more important (as in: already famous / successful / proven) careers to plan.

"It's all about making *you* more you," Adrienne said, pointing at Emily with a forkful of egg white. "What you've got besides talent is authenticity. People respond to that." Mac nodded again, typing *authenticity* into her phone. Adrienne continued. "It's your *essence.*" Emily didn't know why Mac and Adrienne put so much emphasis on something that was *invisible*. But according to Mac and Adrienne, an essence was just as obvious as hair color or height, the second you walked into a room.

Emily's mind was spinning with all the ways she needed to be a better Emily. She peeked at Mac's screen and read the notes thus far:

1. Start reading scripts—get E copies of *Little Miss Hamlet* and *Running in Alaska.*
2. Talk to Valerie Waters—training regimen? Too soon?
3. Remind A to talk to Warner Bros.
4. Have generals with the top 20 casting directors. E has to meet Sheila Darrow!
5. Headshots—is Scarlett's photographer still on Abbott-Kinney?
6. Consult with Xochi—branding her image.
7 Hire a PR agency—call Cardammon re: Lindsy Smith-Zelman.
8. Acting class. Is Larry Moss taking new students?
9. Authenticity!

While Mac was busy taking notes and Adrienne was fidgeting with her BlackBerry, Emily furtively held up her iPhone and took a picture of Jake. She couldn't wait to show it to Paige, as part of her online L.A. scrapbook.

Mac stopped sipping her smoothie and shot Emily a *don't do that again* stare.

Emily shrugged.

"No, seriously, sweetie," Mac said, speaking for the first time that breakfast. "If you want to fit in here, you cannot get excited every time you see a celeb, okay?"

"Well, she *can* get excited, Mac," Adrienne corrected her. "She just can't play paparazzi."

"The only stars you can get excited about are the cult heroes," Mac said, as though it were common knowledge. She took a sip of her smoothie. "Quentin Tarantino, Philip Seymour Hoffman, Meryl Streep—you know what I mean?"

"Even PSH is too mainstream," Adrienne observed, fluffing her reddish blond bob, "but definitely Quentin."

Emily couldn't believe this mother-daughter duo were sitting at a table arguing about how much enthusiasm you could show when you saw a real, live movie star.

"Got it," Emily said with a brisk nod, wanting to end this lecture already.

Adrienne took one last sip of her cappuccino and dropped her BlackBerry into her alligator-skin Birkin bag. "I love your energy," Adrienne sighed wistfully. "I haven't felt this way since Katie Bosworth arrived."

Emily smiled. She had never been compared to Kate

Bosworth, but it was definitely a compliment. Especially coming from someone who actually *knew* "Katie."

Adrienne leaned into the table and focused her steely blue gaze on Emily. It was the first time all morning that she'd actually made eye contact. "And listen, I hate to dip into the clichés about Hollywood, but here goes: At the end of the day, it's not who you know. It's not even who knows you." Her BlackBerry was buzzing again. She reached down to retrieve it, still piercing Emily with her laserlike eye contact. She pointed the device at Emily like a sword. "This town is all about who knows you and who *adores* you."

Emily swallowed her lemon-infused mineral water. The idea of making people adore her was scary. There wasn't a coach for *that*.

Adrienne's eyes darted across the screen, reading her latest work e-mail. Then she stood abruptly. If it had been anyone else, the sudden movements would have signaled an emergency, but Adrienne just operated in a semipermanent state of 911.

Apparently breakfast was over.

Adrienne dropped the girls off at BAMS at 7:35 a.m. exactly. She had an 8 a.m. meeting at Initiative, and—as Emily knew from every Hollywood magazine profile she'd read about her—Adrienne Little-Armstrong was never late.

The girls stood at the end of the BAMS driveway, in

the cul-de-sac where parents and nannies dropped off kids, staring down at the school's wide-open, wrought-iron gates, where one navy blue Team Mac banner hung loosely, flapping in the breeze. Emily could feel the other kids staring at Mac, sizing up her every move. Emily was admiring the Mac-frenzy when a familiar Rolls-Royce Phantom slid by the curb.

"Let's go make sure Team Tachman *adores* you," Mac said lazily. She flipped on her Gucci aviators and buttoned up her Ron Herman cashmere cardigan. "This is gonna rock," she added in a sarcastic voice. Mac always looked upon Kimmie interactions as a chore, even though the girl was just slightly dorky and tried a tad too hard. But, as Mac had already explained, everyone had to be kind of nice to Kimmie, because everyone's parents wanted to work with her dad.

Mac and Emily stepped to the side of the Rolls-Royce. They waited while Kimmie stepped out, reached into the backseat for her white oversize Coach bag, and then shut the door.

"'Sup, Mac," Kimmie said, pulling her bag onto her shoulder. Emily opened her mouth to say hello, but before she could get the word out, Kimmie turned away. "HeyEmilysorryI'minarush," she said as she darted off toward Main Quad.

Emily glanced at her Swatch. It was still only seven thirty-eight. So why the rush to get to an eight o'clock class? She shot a confused glance at Mac.

But Mac was useless at the moment—she'd started talking to a boy Emily instantly recognized as Lukas Gregory. Mac had already prepped Emily on all the cute boys. Just as Mac had described, he had dark hair and dark eyes, and the kind of perfect, all-natural tan that came from playing water polo in BAMS's outdoor pool two hours a day. According to Mac, he'd spent the summer with his family in Tuscany, where he'd joined a local water polo team and learned to speak Italian. Mac was laughing and eyeing Lukas as though he were a new window display at Ron Herman.

Emily stayed put, wanting to give Mac some space. Maybe the Kimmie brush-off was nothing, she told herself. After all, Kimmie *had* said hello. Just not in that usual overeager puppy-dog way she usually said hello. Emily had read how people moved to L.A. and became super paranoid about everything. She shivered—was L.A. already making her crazy?

The Phantom was lurking in the driveway with the engine running. She looked up and spotted the famous producer staring at her through his rearview mirror. Actually, he was *glaring*. Emily looked at Mac for help, but Mac and Lukas were now watching a YouTube clip on Mac's iPhone. Emily doubled-checked and confirmed on her own: Elliot *was* glaring.

Does he think I blew off his daughter? Is he wondering why I haven't said hello to him? Remembering Adrienne's breakfast advice, Emily pushed up the sleeves of her teal

Forever 21 hoodie, pushed her bangs out of her eyes, and stepped forward to show Elliot her positive energy. After all, she was supposed to have a meeting with him next week to discuss a role he'd handpicked for her. She might as well build their relationship now.

"Hi, Mr. Tachman!" Emily chirped. "Good to see you!" The second she heard herself she wanted to hit delete. She sounded so fake, like she was trying way too hard. The "Desperado" song played in her head, the sound track to her life at that second.

Elliot glared at Emily through his thin, rectangular glasses. She had never noticed how large his head was until that moment. He started to roll up the window. Just before the tinted glass slid all the way up, he said in an eerily calm voice, "Excuse me—I have a meeting." And then he drove off, leaving Emily to wonder what had just happened.

Emily spun around on her checkerboard Vans to face Mac who, at that moment, was putting a Team Mac pin on Lukas's black Fred Perry polo shirt. "You have to wear it all day!" Mac said, fake-seriously.

"Matches my shirt, huh?" Lukas patted the pin. "Laters," he said, and gave a lazy head-nod to Mac as he walked off to class.

Emily waited until Lukas was out of earshot before she leaned into Mac and whispered, "Did I do something wrong?"

"What are you talking about?" Mac asked, still smiling

from her Lukas encounter. She blinked her eyes twice as if to snap away the giddiness.

"E-Tach wasn't very friendly to me. He just blew me off."

Mac rolled her eyes. "What do you want? A goodie bag every time E-Tach sees you?"

"No, I didn't mean that," Emily stammered, suddenly embarrassed. Maybe this was just how Bel-Air worked. In Iowa, friends' parents didn't roll up a window and drive away when you greeted them politely. But here, people were always rushing off places.

Mac started to type an e-mail on her iPhone. "Have you forgotten that Elliot Tachman is *the* most important man in this town?" she said without looking up. "He has more meetings in a day than most people have in a lifetime. You're lucky if he talks to you."

Emily smiled and decided to act as though she felt better. Maybe then her emotions would catch up. But when she mentally rewound the memory and played it back, all she could remember was Elliot's stony stare. It was a very negative *essence*.

As Emily watched his sleek black car glide down the redbrick driveway like a funeral car, she felt a death-knot in her stomach. Even though Emily was brand-new to Bel-Air, she didn't need Mac or Adrienne to explain that being on Elliot Tachman's bad side was a very bad place to be.

CHAPTER seven

COCO

◄ Wednesday September 9 ►

7 AM	Last-minute shopping for dance mtg brekkie
7:55 AM	Meet Mom to get my iPod (must do bag check before I leave the house!)
8 AM	Dance mtg
12 PM	Vote for Mac!
6:30 PM	Have we figured out where we're celebrating MASC (Mac As Social Chair)? I suggest Katsuya. Double check SpoiledinLA website to be sure

Coco was still on a high from yesterday's first dance practice as she bounded down the gray stone steps to the Clubhouse, the little café reserved exclusively for BAMS activity groups. It was a pine-colored wooden shack that served espresso drinks and homemade chocolate chip cookies. Attached was a terrace with white iron tables and a view overlooking Stone Canyon.

This morning was Coco's first meeting as dance captain, and Coco was half an hour early because she wanted to have breakfast waiting for the girls when they arrived. She had read in the *New York Times* that people did best at meetings when there was food. Which was why Coco held baskets of Bagel Broker bagels (for the girls who still ate carbs), containers of Stonyfield Farm cottage cheese (for the girls who were off carbs), and Susina Bakery croissants (for the girls who still ate good food). Coco's mind had been so abuzz preparing for the meeting that she'd forgotten her mini Bose speakers on the marble fireplace back home. She'd intended to use them (along with her handy little iPod nano) to get the girls pepped up despite the early hour. Luckily her mom was headed that way and was going to bring her speakers to BAMS, just in time for her meeting.

It was amazing how much could happen in a week, Coco thought, as she clicked down the slate steps in her Lanvin ankle boots. Ruby was on the injured list, and "far too busy" to come to practices, as she'd announced in an e-mail to the team—which Coco knew meant she was too proud to sit and watch Coco act as captain. But without Ruby, the team was so much happier than last year. Coco felt better not having to wonder what her archrival thought of every choice she made.

Coco couldn't stop thinking about how great practice had been the day before: The girls seemed to be really excited that she was captain, and they'd agreed upon the routine for the fund-raiser in *twenty-three minutes* (a new BAMS record! Historically it took several hours, many meetings, and a few tear-jerking sessions for the Bam-Bams to agree on anything). The choice had been so simple because the girls wanted to use Coco's choreography from her audition for their performance at ExtravaBAMSa. (A huge compliment!) Haylie was still being a pain, but Coco knew that no one really took Haylie seriously, and that any self-confidence the girl had was probably a temporary ego boost from her sketchy membership in the Thinner Circle.

Fund-raising Day, better known as ExtravaBAMSa, was Coco's favorite event of the year. It was a daylong showcase of the school's world-class athletes and artists. Mac always joked that it was just a reminder to parents why BAMS was worth the tuition—they paid a hefty sum to have their children surrounded by excellence. Because the groups really *were* excellent: The culinary club had a cook-off, the thespian society—run by Kimmie Tachman—put on a one-act play, the surf team put on an exhibition, and of course the Bam-Bams performed, all in the name of raising gazillions of dollars for the charity voted on by the BAMS student body. This year's cause was Save Darfur.

As Coco's patent leather ankle boots landed on the last step to the terrace, she was thinking about where she could get her little speakers set up so they wouldn't get drowned out—she was excited to play "Umbrella" for the girls and talk about ways to tweak her routine for a group show. She looked up to check the status of the gazebo and then gasped—all eight dance team members were already there, sitting at the white iron tables in their black Lululemon workout pants and navy dance team hoodies. They stopped talking when Coco arrived. In eerie silence, she observed the scattering of mostly empty glasses of orange juice and a few scraps of toast on people's plates.

Coco checked the time on her iPhone. It was definitely twenty minutes *before* the meeting was supposed to start. *So why were they already finishing up?* Coco set the ginormous baskets of food on the ground. She stood there, wondering what was going on and how long it would take for someone to acknowledge her. This was definitely not a good sign.

"Oh, hiyeee, Coco!" Haylie Fowler baby-talked. She always sounded like she was delivering bad news. Haylie pushed back her white iron chair, stood up, and walked over to face Coco, her rectangular body blocking the view of the canyon and the sunlight. She was wearing a trucker hat turned sideways and an ill-fitting wifebeater. Somehow she'd missed the memo that the Tara Reid look was so 5Y (five years ago). And even then it hadn't worked.

Coco gulped, feeling like an animal about to be killed. The fact that Haylie Fowler, aka SSD, was about to tell Coco what was going on with the Bam-Bams, in front of the whole dance team, was beyond a bad sign.

"I guess we forgot to tell you. . . ." Haylie trailed off. She cocked her head to the side and looked at Coco with a fake pout, as though that explained everything. "Oh?" Coco said, pursing her lips. She couldn't bear to look at Haylie's squinty eyes. She looked around the terrace, scanning the faces of her friends. Lucia, Maribel, and Taylor's lips were pursed, their faces stony. They looked massively uncomfortable, like they were staring at smog over the Hollywood Hills in August. Eden twirled her fork. They all looked guilty. The knot in Coco's stomach tightened. "What did you forget to tell me, Haylie?"

"Oh, just, you know . . . that we changed the time and stuff."

Changed the time? Without her? "Actually, Haylie, I'm the *captain*. I need to know about this," Coco said, trying to hit that note between scolding and making a point. "Someone needs to call me next time." She spoke calmly but her heart was doing pirouettes.

There was a long beat of silence during which Coco could feel everyone looking at her. The only sound was the chirping of black parakeets in the canyon. She took a sip of her Voss water to calm herself down.

Haylie scrunched her face up as though Coco had just picked her nose. "Um, actually, Coco, you might want to go easy on that?"

"Go easy on what?" Coco asked, taking another sip. The other girls giggled. Coco wondered if she'd accidentally spilled on her shirt. She looked down, but it was all clear. She wiped her nose to make sure there was nothing gross hanging out.

Haylie shook her head. "Never mind. We all have our issues." She took a deep breath. "Actually, Coco, what I really wanted to say is that, due to creative differences, we kinda had a re-vote," Haylie whined. Coco's heart beat wildly. *Re-vote?* Haylie's pale face was scrunched, like she'd bitten into a lemon. "And, long story short, um . . . I'm kind of the captain."

"Is this *kind of* a joke?" Coco glanced around the terrace frantically, trying to lock eyes with Lucia and then Maribel, and then Taylor or Eden. Lucia was stirring her coffee, her legs and arms crossed so that she looked like a pretzel. Maribel stared into her lap, her head hung low in shame. Eden looked out at the canyon. Taylor was robotically coating her lips in Burt's Bees. The other girls were looking down into their empty water cups, pretending to be fascinated by the clear plastic.

Coco felt like someone had squeezed the air out of her. She knew it would be too unkind to scream what she was thinking, which was *BUT YOU ARE THE WORST DANCER ON THIS TEAM. WE CALL YOU SEVEN-SECOND DELAY!* Instead she decided the only safe choice was to stare until SSD said something that made sense.

Haylie played with the yellow Lance Armstrong bracelets on her chubby arms, shying away from eye contact. "I'm sorry, Coco," she said, tilting her hat even more sideways, and sounding not at all sorry. "But there's a bright side. Even though you're no longer captain, we've discussed this." She put her hands on her hips. "You can still totally be on the team. As alternate." She smiled, a little too gleefully. Coco felt as though she'd been hit with a stun gun. Everyone—and *especially* Haylie—knew alternates didn't perform. Coco might as well have had one leg: That was all you needed to be an alternate.

Coco scanned the terrace again, hoping for a friendly face, but everyone was quiet. The team's silence hurt the most, since apparently they had all *discussed* her moments ago. It was never, ever a good feeling to know that you had been *discussed*. She rubbed her lucky Macedonian sun necklace, a gift from her father when he'd opened his Athens hotel, summoning her courage.

"I joined this team to *dance,*" Coco said carefully. "So if I can't do that, I quit." She spun on her Lanvin heels, willing herself not to cry. Without another word, she ran up the stone trail to the BAMS driveway, past the new bonsai trees dotting the path.

At the top of the stairs, she spotted her mom's pale blue Bentley with its super-tinted windows. Coco's mother was waiting for her in the driveway, and Coco had never been so delighted to have forgotten something at home. Behind the car was a cluster of paparazzi on motorcycles. Two years earlier, Cardammon had been given a strict warning from the BAMS headmaster about bringing reporters to school. But she'd agreed to stay away from campus during school hours to keep BAMS tabloid-free.

Except for emergencies, like when Coco forgot mini speakers.

Coco grabbed the car door handle, emblazoned with all of her family members' initials, CK, in bright gold. She slunk inside the car and leaned against the tan leather seat, shutting her eyes.

Cardammon removed Coco's little speakers from her Yves Saint Laurent snakeskin satchel. "Luvvy, here you go!" she said proudly, as though she'd helped deliver a newborn baby. With her tan face, high cheekbones, and perfect ski jump nose, Cardammon looked more like Coco's older sister than her mother. She handed over the device, her sparkly orange fingernails glittering in the sunlight. The orange polish perfectly matched Cardammon's tight satin jumpsuit and her orange feather-brimmed fedora. She looked like a sexy astronaut.

Coco stared at her mother, baffled by the latest ensemble. "Mum, are you going somewhere?" *Like the moon?*

"Not at all," Cardammon said, sounding surprised at the question. For a second Coco forgot her pain and laughed to herself at her mother's free-spiritedness. No wonder people around the world loved her.

"Thanks for this, Mum," Coco said. She sank down into her seat so that the paparazzi couldn't see her. Even though the windows were tinted, she couldn't take any chances that they'd get a shot of her looking the way she felt that moment.

Cardammon's thin lips curled into a smile and her coffee-colored eyes twinkled. She always looked a little naughty. "Luvvy, I just want to say that I am so proud of you, my little captain." She looked like she was about to pinch Coco's cheeks, but Cardammon was *not* that kind of mother.

The second Coco heard the word *captain*, her pain pounced back on her. She quickly wiped away her teardrops before her mother could notice them slipping onto her cheeks. She did not want to have to explain any of this drama to her mother, who wouldn't understand. Megastardom came so easily to Cardammon, and Coco couldn't even stay on her *middle school* dance team. Had she gotten all the bad genes?

"I was worried that I'd been pushing too hard with the record deal," Cardammon said, rubbing her slender hands with Fresh sugar-blossom hand cream. "And then you go off getting elected captain by your friends. And really—what's more important than the respect of your peers? My Grammys mean more to me than my MTV Awards or my platinums," she sighed.

Coco cringed. There was no sense in pointing out the colossal difference in their situations, namely that Cardammon was a huge success and she was a total loser. "Mom, you weren't pushing me too hard. I wanted to be a pop star," Coco said. It was the truth. "And about the dance team—"

"Shushie, luvvy! You just focus on your team. I can't wait to see you dance at the fund-raiser. We'll raise lots of dosh for those Africans! Even your father's coming!"

"Dad's coming?" Coco squeaked. It was unusual for Charles Kingsley to stay in the same country for more than two weeknights, and now she'd have to disappoint *two* parents. That news flash zapped any remaining strength to explain that she'd been booted out of her captainship. She scooted even lower in her seat to make sure that the paparazzi couldn't get a glimpse of her.

"I should get going," Coco muttered, afraid she'd start crying if she stayed. She just couldn't believe she had failed so quickly. What could she possibly say to her mom?

Cardammon looked down at her D&G diamond-studded wristwatch. "Right! Back to your meeting! Go, go, go!" She waved Coco out with her orange-tipped fingernails, the scent of her sugar-blossom lotion wafting through the car.

Coco covered her face with her arms, knowing the exact angle to position them so that none of the photographers could get her running back to school. Pictures of Coco were worth a lot—Cardammon had sold her baby pictures to *Hello!* for a cool million and donated the money to a pediatric AIDS foundation. The last thing Coco wanted was for the paparazzi to catch a picture of her crying. She imagined the headlines: CARDAMMON'S CRYBABY DAUGHTER: FOREVER BLUE.

Once Coco was inside the BAMS gates, she ran through Main Quad, past the awkward girls with sketchbooks, to a lonely wooden bench overlooking the Stone Canyon Reservoir. She clutched her tiny speakers, knowing she wouldn't need *those* anymore. In the distance, a deer darted under a tree. Coco inhaled the crisp scent of the eucalyptus trees and let the tears fall.

CHAPTER EIGHT

becks

◀ Wednesday September 9 ▶

8 AM	School's on
12 PM	Vote for Mac
2:55 PM	School's out!
3:47 PM	See Austin!!! (Where will our date be??? And yes, everyone, I promise a full report aysap the second it's over)

Becks strolled into the BAMS food hall to cast her vote for Mac as social chair, bouncing in step to Fergie's "Fergalicious," which was blasting in her Bose headphones. She was wearing her blue and white nautical striped Splendid tee, Hudson jeans, a rhinestone-studded belt, and Havaiana flip-flops that showed off her cotton candy pink pedicure. The outfit had been specifically chosen in preparation for her *après*-school date that day with Austin. (T minus three hours and forty-seven minutes!) Becks had actually packed Maybelline lash expansion mascara (!), Stellar Strawberry lip shimmer (!!), and a hairbrush (!!!) so that she could *brush her hair* and *primp* before she saw Austin. All of which was a serious effort.

The food hall was designed to look like a giant alpine ski chalet, with pale wooden beams that held up the triangular roof. Becks was headed to the center, to drop off her ballot for Mac as social chair in the giant silver voting box, which was placed atop the picnic table. But she was on autopilot: All she could think about was Austin.

Social chair ballots had been distributed in homeroom earlier that morning, and voting was very simple: You ripped off one end of the ballot—the navy side to vote for Mac, and the silver portion to vote for Ruby. Becks ripped the navy half and dropped it into the box, which was guarded by the head of student council, Elsa Peters, a pale brunette girl who always asked people their grades and was already obsessed with getting into college.

As Becks turned to head back outside, she spotted some fellow surf team members: Caitlin Pressley and Fisher Maxwell. Caitlin was a tomboy who was very well liked because she always, sincerely had something nice to say about everyone. Fisher was her best friend, and everyone called him "Tailgate" because he followed Caitlin everywhere. Becks high-fived them, but she didn't take off her headphones to chitchat.

On a normal, non-date-with-Austin day, Becks would have mingled with her teammates and spied on the voters, trying to gauge how Mac was doing. Instead she was thinking about how to greet Austin (a hug or a high five?), where they might be going (surfing or a movie?), and how she would feel (tingly and excited? Or pukey and nervous?) when she actually got to see him again. Hopefully she wouldn't blush too much. It felt like they'd been apart forever, even though it had only been forty-two and a half hours. Not that she was counting.

Becks was so absorbed in her Austin daydreaming that she didn't even realize Ellie Parker had been walking right beside her. Becks pushed the door to head outside, and felt a tiny hand on her arm.

"Heeey, Becks! Earth to Becks!" Ellie let go of Becks and snapped her fingers. Even Becks could tell she had very obvio-acrylic nails. How 818. Becks let go of the door and took out her headphones.

Ellie's long blond hair was blown out in waves à la Ruby's 1970s style, and her skin was the exact shade of a Creamsicle, just like Ruby's. She looked like she could be Heidi Montag's baby sister. Ellie wore a white tunic top with hip-hugger jeans and a Lance Armstrong bracelet on each tiny wrist. Ruby and her friends were starting to look, dress, and talk exactly the same: *Rubybots*. Becks imagined a Rubybot factory, complete with assembly line and conveyor belt, churning out fake girls with fake blond hair and fake tans.

"How are you!" Ellie said. It was not a question.

"Hey Ellie," Becks muttered, wondering why Ellie was even talking to her. Something about Ellie's girly-girliness always made Becks feel like a dude. "What's up?"

"Actually, I was thinking. . . ." Ellie twirled a bleached blond lock of hair around her finger. She used the same baby-talk voice as Ruby. "Maybe we could hang out later? Grab some Pinkberry?"

Becks scanned Ellie's angelic face, searching for clues as to why Ellie would suddenly want to spend time with her. She flashed back to the last time they'd "hung out"—when Ellie had flirted like crazy with Austin on the beach. Becks couldn't stop a smug smile from spreading across her face. Or from blurting out, "Actually, I'm busy today. I'm hanging out with *Austin*." She looked right at Ellie challengingly.

If Ellie was the tiniest bit jealous, she didn't show it. In fact, she seemed amused. "Booooo," Ellie said. "But yummeee for you!"

"I guess so." Becks shrugged. Ellie was so weird. Trying to understand her was like trying to understand Nicole Richie's fame: pointless. Becks threw her orange and black North Face backpack over her right shoulder and headed outside.

"Maybe some other time!" Ellie called after her.

Becks nodded and waved goodbye without turning around. Just as she entered the sunlit courtyard, she felt her phone vibrate in her Hudson jeans pocket.

It was a text.

From Austin.

Becks almost dropped the phone when she read the message:

CANT MAKE IT 2DAY.

Her hand trembled and her heart sank. *Why was he bailing?* She stared at the phone desperately, wishing he'd written more. Maybe it was just a boy thing to give bad text?

She took a deep breath to get Zen and typed her response.

NP! TMRW?

Becks stood in the courtyard, staring at her phone while people bumped into her, rushing to class. Becks ambled forward, her gaze fixed on the screen. She had exactly three minutes until Mandarin Chinese class, and she needed to get centered, fast.

Becks inhaled deeply through her nostrils and blew out the air as though she were blowing through an imaginary straw. It had worked that summer before she surfed the Pipeline in Hawaii. She lifted up her left leg to focus on her balance on her right leg—to concentrate on anything but her panicky confusion. She was standing in tree pose by one of the Main Quad arches when her phone buzzed again. She grabbed it from her jeans pocket like she was gasping for air.

SRY NO. VRY BZY L8TLY.

Becks shook her phone frantically as though it were a Magic 8 Ball, staring at Austin's non-words on her screen. Apparently she wasn't even worth a full "S-O-R-R-Y." The only *real* word he'd taken the time to write was *no*.

O-U-C-H.

Becks turned her phone off and dropped it into her backpack. She needed to de-text for a while. But even though the phone was out of sight, she could still see Austin's mysterious message running on loop in her mind. What had happened in the past forty-two hours and thirty-seven minutes to make him change his mind?

Becks wiped the lip shimmer off her face like it was poison. She wouldn't need *that* today.

CHAPTER nine

mac

◀ Wednesday September 9 ▶

TODAY: Social chair elections

3:05 PM SCE Results

6:30 PM Celebrate SCE victory with I.C.! (Nobu or Katsuya? Or Violet? I'm w/ Co, leaning toward Katsuya, but B & E, you need to weigh in!)

Mac put her purple Mulberry Mabel bag down carefully on La Table in Main Quad. She was trying to carry the bare minimum at all times and avoid being weighed down by a backpack, which was so public school.

To anyone who didn't know BAMS, La Table was just an ordinary wooden picnic table, carved with initials and hearts. But it had been the Inner Circle's *après*-school headquarters since day one of middle school. It was located perfectly in the center of Main Quad, an eighth-grade microcosm where you could see all the BAMS cliques. At that moment, Mac had an excellent view of the soccer boys, the awkward girls who were already starting their homework, and the quirky kids who were a little too into blue tights.

Mac reached into her bag to quickly reapply some Chanel Waterlily lip gloss while pretending not to look around her. She spotted Lukas and Hunter playing

Hacky Sack on the field. She arched her shoulders back for a glam position, just in case they caught a glimpse of her looking so effortlessly cute in her Team Mac T-shirt, Rock & Republic jeans, and Mella flip-flops. She hoped they had voted for her. She imagined how she would just "happen" to walk by Lukas right after the all-school e-mail landed announcing the new social chair, and how it would feel when he hugged her. *Not* that she was crushing on him or anything. She had much more important things to do than worry about a *boy.* She discreetly spritzed some Vera Wang Princess on her wrist just in case.

Mac was *thisclose* to achieving her dream-of-all-dreams, and she just wanted to not totally freak out. She held her phone above her head and snapped an appearance-check picture. She flinched when she saw her photo. She looked haggard and tired, like the "Stars Without Their Makeup!" pictures in the back of magazines. Except that Mac *was* wearing makeup. Yes, camera phones could deceive, but they weren't vicious lie-mongers.

Clearly this was Life telling Mac to take better care of herself. She decided to begin with her tan. Mac hopped off La Table and onto the bench. She closed her eyes, leaned back, and let the sun do its magic. (But not for more than four minutes, or she'd do sun damage.)

Mac had racked up a minute of vitamin D rays when she heard Emily's voice. It was laced with panic.

"E-Tach's definitely mad at me," Emily hissed.

Mac opened her eyes and realized that Emily, Becks, and Coco were huddled around her, like she'd just fainted. They were all talking over each other.

"Austin blew me off," Becks wailed.

"They said I can't be captain," Coco said frantically.

"'Cause he rolled up his window on me!" Emily yelped.

"But why would I be an *alternate*?" Coco howled.

"And I have no idea why!" Becks's voice cracked.

Soon it was just a nonsensical earthquake of words.

"Unfair!"

"Blows!"

"Why me?"

Before Mac could get into it, she felt a buzz in her pocket. She held up her phone like a white flag to her friends. "It's Ruby."

There was insta-silence. The last time Ruby had e-mailed Mac it had been to tell her that Emily had lost a starring role in a major Hollywood movie.

The girls tightened the circle so there was no daylight, and they leaned in to peer at Mac's screen.

To: Mac.Littlearmstrong@bams.edu
From: Ruby.Goldman@bams.edu
Subject: SAW THIS ON INTRANET THOUGHT U MIGHT ENJOY XOXO RG

"Let's just see what this is," Mac said calmly, clicking on the link. She turned her iPhone horizontally and an online movie began to play. Mac's nerves fired up when the credits flashed, in the exact same Courier font that Mac had used for her Team Mac T-shirts:

"Le Slumber Party"

Starring:

MACKENZIE LITTLE-FARTSTRONG as the girl who is 2 cool 4 school!

EVANGELINA BECKS as the girl who hearts Pinkberry! (A little too much!)

CORDELIA "COCO" KINGSLEY as the girl you can Depends on!

And introducing EMILY MUNGLER as Cat Girl! Or is that Brat Girl?

Rated U for Unbelievable!

Mac's heart stopped for a moment and her breath came in short, staccato bursts as she put together the bizarre clues like a CSI detective: Pinkberry . . . Cat Girl . . . Depends. Suddenly, it clicked: *They were talking about the Inner Circle slumber party!* On the tiny screen, Emily appeared, doing her catlike imitation of Kimmie Tachman. Mac's mind raced back to the prank they'd played on Ruby, and then she remembered with a jaw-dropping jolt: She had never logged out of the iChat! Everything that they'd done after that prank would have been recorded if the person on the other end hadn't logged off. And of course Ruby had lurked.

Mac looked at her friends, her throat drier than a Palm Springs cactus. Emily was ghostly pale, Coco looked like she was going to faint, and Becks was too angry to speak. Everyone's face seemed to say the same thing: *Whose fault was it?*

"Oh, jeez, did I mix that up?" Emily asked, her hands on her cheeks.

"No, it's my fault," Mac said numbly, staring down at her phone. "I put you up to that in the first place." Mac's mind was throbbing. How, she wondered, could she have been so careless? This was such an *amateur* move.

Mac pressed play again, and the video smash-cut to Becks and Coco chanting, in unison, "KIMMIE TACHMAN!" The impression had seemed funny at the time, but now it just looked mean, like the girls had nothing better to do than make fun of people. Clearly Ruby hadn't just whipped up the video on her laptop. This monstrosity had been professionally edited.

"But Ems made fun of us, too!" Becks said, pointing a shaky finger at the screen. "She didn't just make fun of Kimmie!"

"And we said nice things about Kimmie!" Coco wailed, wrapping her lithe arms around her body in a self-protective hug. "Ruby cut out all that."

"How do we know it was Ruby?" Emily asked innocently. Her eyes were wide open in horror and her leg was shaking. She looked like she was about to topple over.

Becks and Coco shook their heads, as if to say, *Poor little thing*.

"Welcome to BAMS," Mac said sarcastically.

But the video wasn't over. Next there was Becks's Pinkberry disaster. She leaned over her yogurt. "Pretend this is Austin," she cooed. And there she was, slobbering all over her Pinkberry, looking insane and gross.

"Oh no," Becks whispered, pressing her hands to her heart. "I'm gonna be sick."

The next shot was of Coco, squeezing her legs, and Mac pointing out that she'd peed herself. Mac realized that the background "music" was actually an overlay of farting sounds. And then there was Mac's voice, saying, "I'm lactose intolerant."

The denouement was Mac's declaration, "Even after I win social chair I'm still going to hang out with you girls all the time. I have no interest in hanging out with anyone else at BAMS." Ruby had actually *subtitled* this bit of dialogue so there could be no mistaking Mac's conceitedness. As the girls screamed, "Tell us something we don't know!!!" and laughed hysterically, everyone looked snobby by association.

Finally, THE END popped up. The screen went black.

Mac's veins were pulsing out of her body. "It's THE END all right." She dropped her phone on the picnic table. The video was making her ache all over.

"So everyone at BAMS knows I peed my pants!" Coco spoke softly, staring at the phone like it was a dead body.

"And that I make out with fro-yo!" Becks said, her hands pressed against her eyes as if to keep them closed. "Austin must have seen it and canceled our date!"

"That's why Haylie asked if I should be drinking water . . ." Coco mumbled.

"And they all think we hate them," Emily said sadly, pointing out the far bigger problem. She pushed her cinnamon brown bangs behind her ear.

"I feel so violated," Mac said. Her sleepover—a private moment just for the Inner Circle—had been judged by the entire school. It was Mac's worst nightmare times the BAMS population (352). She revised her thoughts on Internet safety. *Rule number one: Always log off.*

"We're destroyed," Coco said flatly.

Hearing Coco say that, Mac felt a huge weight on her shoulders, knowing that she had caused this problem for everyone. After all, it had been *her* idea to prank Ruby. It was *her* fault for not logging off her own stupid computer. It was *her* big mouth that had made them all look like conceited snobs. Mac *had* to fix this.

Just then, Ruby hobbled over to Le Table on her shiny titanium crutches, wearing white Ralph Lauren trousers and a silky white Nanette Lepore top. Dressed in all white with her crutches, she looked like a mad scientist with metallic arms. She was flanked by her Rubybots: Ellie, Haylie, and Kimmie, whose looks had all evidently been hijacked by the same stylist, given their new uniform of jeans, flowy tunics, flip-flops, and Orange County tans. Ruby stopped a hobble away from the girls and smiled an evil grin.

"Are you girls okay?" she asked, faking innocence. She smiled slyly over at the Rubybots, who smiled back obediently, as if on cue.

"Oh, I wonder, Little Miss Filmmaker," Mac hissed. "Sofia Coppola better watch out."

"I have no idea what you're talking about," Ruby cooed. She shot yet another sly smile over at the Rubybots, who smiled back.

"Save it for the DVD," Mac snapped angrily. If she stayed angry, then at least she wouldn't cry. "Everyone knows you leaked that video."

Ruby tapped her chin with her index finger, pretending to think. "Oh, the link I sent you that I found online? I did see it. It was so . . . interesting." She shrugged, as if she were bored of talking about it. "Here's a prezzie for you," Ruby said, handing Mac one of the yellow Lance Armstrong bracelets that everyone at BAMS was wearing. "In case you need more stuff with your name on it," Ruby laughed. Then she hobbled off, her entourage triumphantly trailing after her.

Mac looked down at the bracelet, wondering what in the world Ruby was up to. Then she realized instead of LIVESTRONG, the bracelet had been custom-made to say FARTSTRONG. She dropped it like it was a trans fat.

Mac shuddered, wondering how many people had been wearing this atrocity, making fun of her all day. She hadn't even noticed. Missing the obvious was the worst feeling of all. She looked around the quad and realized BAMS students were checking out La Table like drivers checking out an accident on the 405 Freeway. Mac looked up and took in the scene: She spotted the baseball boys. The fake-goth twins. Even Hunter and Lukas (oh no!). It seemed like everyone was wearing a yellow bracelet. And suddenly La Table—at the center of it all—seemed like the worst place to be. Mac inhaled very slowly, knowing that these people probably hated her for her cruel remarks. Mac would have hated herself too.

Coco was staring at the ground and hugging herself, and Emily was rapidly twirling a lock of hair around her index finger while her right leg bounced nervously. Becks was standing on one leg taking deep breaths that sounded like borderline sobbing.

From the table, Mac's phone buzzed, breaking the eerie silence. Emily and Coco realized their phones were buzzing as well.

Becks reached down to pick up Mac's phone. She

checked the screen quickly, and then said somberly, "It's an all-school e-mail."

Social chair election results!

"Just tell me what it says," Mac groaned, shielding her eyes with her right hand.

"Sorry, Mac," Becks said sadly. She turned the screen toward Mac so she could read the e-mail herself.

To: All BAMS
From: Headmaster Billingsley
Subject: CONGRATULATIONS TO RUBY GOLDMAN, BAMS'S NEW SOCIAL CHAIR!

CHAPTER TEN

emily

◀ Wednesday September 9 ▶

4:45 PM Pack my bags for Iowa?

6:30 PM Daily iChat w/Paige (I *really* hate iChat)

Emily sat on a padded white chaise longue by the Armstrong's pool, toying with her BFF bangle. She was trying to seem calm while Mac used her iBook's wireless to lurk on the Bel-Air intranet, reading the comments on Slumbergate, as their video scandal had been quickly dubbed. Becks and Coco sat in lounges next to her, looking like people on TV news who'd lost their homes in a fire. They seemed stunned and sad, and like they had nowhere to go.

"How is that even allowed on the Bel-Air intranet?" Becks asked glumly. She took a handful of dried goji berries from the clear bag on her lap. It was a gorgeous Los Angeles afternoon, with dry air and hot sun, and the turquoise Olympic-size pool sparkled invitingly. But nobody had even bothered to change into a swimsuit. Playing in the pool was the sort of thing people did when they were ready to have fun, which probably wasn't going to happen for the Inner Circle anytime soon.

"It's not allowed. But no one can prove Ruby leaked it," Coco pointed out, taking a sip of her Lemogrino, which was a Mac-created blend of San Pellegrino bubbly water, squeezed Meyer lemons, and sugar.

"Well, the good news is that the video's been removed," Mac said, looking up momentarily from her laptop screen. "But the bad news is that it was up there for eight hours."

Becks and Coco looked at each other and groaned. Emily zipped her teal Forever 21 hoodie just to do something with her fingers, which were shaking uncontrollably. She pushed back the cuticle on her index finger.

"We're D-listed," Becks said glumly, kicking her heel against the deck chair.

"More like Z-listed," Coco corrected.

"There's no letter far enough from A to describe us," Mac said, not looking up from her computer.

"Don't say that," Coco snapped.

Mac pointed to the screen. "I'm just reading what Anonymous13 wrote."

Emily wanted to steer the session back to solutions. "Maybe we're not ruined?" she asked hopefully, smiling gently at Mac and the girls.

"You're ruined," Mac said flatly, the way she might say, *It's Tuesday.* "Kimmie told E-Tach you made fun of her. Ergo you're blacklisted."

Emily's whole body was shaking, like she'd had ten Moroccan mint tea lattes. She squeezed the cushy lounge chair pillows just to calm down. Why had she ever agreed to move to Bel-Air? It was officially the worst decision of her entire life. She could be home in Iowa right now, doing homework with Paige and watching *Access Hollywood* instead of living her own *E! True Hollywood Story.*

Mac's turquoise eyes narrowed into slits. "Oh, look, it's an all-school e-mail from Ruby."

"No more Ruby!" Coco whined, covering her eyes, but she couldn't help but look.

The girls stood up from their chaises and walked behind Mac so they could see her computer screen. Mac clicked on the video link, and a tiny square popped into her screen. It was Ruby, in a red knit dress, her hair tousled Ashley Olsen bed-head style.

From the video screen, Ruby spoke in a soft voice. "First of all, I would like to give a sincere and heartfelt thank-you to everyone at BAMS for voting for me and entrusting me with the responsibility of social chair." Ruby sounded like she was reading off a teleprompter. She was a terrible actress, Emily decided. Nothing she said sounded sincere or heartfelt.

"I could almost *wet my pants* to tell you about what's in store with me as social chair." She grinned wickedly. "First of all, we have a new exclusive contract with *Pinkberry* for the food hall. And for those of you who are *lactose intolerant*"—Ruby actually winked at the computer screen—"we'll be serving a sorbet option." She smiled smugly. "I am so proud to be your elected social chair. Thank you so much. Here's to another great year at BAMS!" She shrugged her shoulders, *aw shucks* style, and the screen went black.

Emily glanced at Mac, who was staring openmouthed at the computer, looking defeated. If Mac was crushed, then how was Emily supposed to have any hope? Nothing about Bel-Air made any sense to her. She didn't even know how to find her locker, let alone find some sense among these ruthless people.

Emily rubbed her temples, wondering if it was too late to sign back up for Cedartown Middle School. She could be on a plane the next day. Sure, it would be uncomfortable to explain to Mac and her mother that she was going home, but in a few hours it would all be forgotten. She could send them a handwritten thank-you note on her Mom's Crane stationery for their effort and interest. She would include a check for the Polo Lounge breakfast. And maybe some nice tuberose soaps from the Bath & Body Works store in the mall.

Emily closed her eyes and imagined being back in Iowa, where she could walk through acres of sunflower fields on her way to school, where kids didn't have their acceptance speeches professionally edited and digitized, and where there was officially zero chance of insulting a legendary producer's daughter and thereby ruining one's own life. She opened her eyes again and stared out at the Armstrongs' shimmering swimming pool. She sort of felt about it the way she did about her Hollywood life: It seemed too good to be true, and just out of reach.

Emily sighed. With hardly a word of goodbye, she slunk away from the girls and dragged her feet upstairs to the guest bedroom to iChat with Paige. She'd officially blown her role as New Girl. And her Hollywood career had ended faster than she could say *Z-list*.

CHAPTER ELEVEN

mac

◀ Wednesday September 9 ▶

5 PM Figure out a way out of this mess

After her friends went home, Mac sat in her bedroom in her green Louis XIV chaise and kicked her heels up on her French-style desk, which she'd had painted the exact same color as her favorite Parisian pastry shop, Hélène. She flipped through a stack of postcards from her friends Emilie and Helene in Paris, wishing she were sipping tea with them at Café de Flore instead of dealing with this fiasco in Bel-Air. But she couldn't stop thinking about Emily. The poor girl had moved all the way from Iowa to have a career. She'd trusted Mac. Now she had nothing.

The doorbell chimed its "Für Elise" ring. Normally Mac ignored the front door, since it was usually messengers or assistants dropping off screenplays or contracts for her parents. But then Mac's phone vibrated. It was a text, from an unknown number:

HEY ITS RUBY. @ YR FRONT DOOR.

Mac winced at her phone like it was a UV ray giving

her wrinkles. It didn't seem like a joke. But if it really was Ruby, what on earth did she want? Hadn't she caused enough pain and suffering? Mac peeked at the security screen on her wall, to see what the front-door cameras picked up. Sure enough, there was Ruby, leaning on her BeDazzled crutches, looking right into the cameras. She was smiling as though she knew Mac was watching. It was like a scene from a horror movie.

Mac tiptoed from her bedroom, down the staircase to the white marble foyer. The door was handcrafted wood, engraved in Bologna, Italy, and it had thick stained-glass panes designed to look like peacocks. Mac angled herself so she could see outside but remain out of Ruby's vision.

Mac's phone buzzed again.

U GOT 5 MINS. LST CHNCE 2 SV YRSLF.

Two texts in a minute. Clearly Ruby wanted something Mac had. *The person who wants something is the person who travels,* Mac reminded herself of one of her mother's pearls of wisdom. Although Mac was very desperate, she was grateful that she still had some cred, though she wasn't sure what exactly that was, or what Ruby could possibly want from her. She waited four minutes and fifty-eight seconds and then flung open the door.

Ruby stood on the front steps, leaning on her shiny crutches, in the same red knit dress she'd worn for her acceptance speech video.

"What do *you* want?" Mac hissed. She spotted Ruby's maid waiting in the circular driveway in a brand-new black Hummer with the engine still running. *Way to watch your carbon footprint!* Mac cringed when she saw the license plate: RUBYRKS. Some poor maid actually had to roll around town in that car.

"I just came by to say hi," Ruby said, smiling brightly, as if it were a normal day after school.

"Hi," Mac said flatly. "And 'bye." She started to close the door.

Ruby put her hand out to stop the door mid-swing and then quickly re-balanced herself on her crutches. "You know, I never did find that assistant. Everyone who applied was a total idiot. And ExtravaBAMSa is the biggest event of fall quarter, and it's just two weeks away."

Mac rolled her eyes, wanting to hear nothing about Ruby's Great Assistant Search or how *she*, not Mac, would be planning ExtravaBAMSa. "What does this have to do with me?" she snapped, staring right into Ruby's big violet eyes. "You're social chair."

"Right, I *am* social chair," Ruby said smugly. "But I'm so busy I don't even have time to run my own life."

"Well, maybe you can hire a life coach?"

Ruby looked at Mac seriously. "Look, people are morons. You're the only person I'd trust to pick out goodie-bag swag. And if you were to interrupt me during my manicure, I'd know it was for a phone call I'd *have* to take." Ruby was trying to seem nonchalant, but in her eyes Mac saw a glimmer of insecurity.

Mac paused to swallow this information. *Ruby wanted Mac to be her assistant*. She was actually standing in Mac's driveway, saying this aloud.

"I got in over my head." Ruby twisted the diamond-studded gold *R* that hung from a long gold chain around her neck. "I've never planned anything before, and I have to choose the menus and the caterers and the decorations. The list goes on and on." Her voice sounded like it was about to crack. "Plus I have to approve all the groups. It's a nightmare, and I can't do it alone."

Mac felt a pang. Before her dreams of being social chair had been shattered, she'd already planned exactly who she would hire for ExtravaBAMSa. Planning parties was something she loved doing, and it required the attention to detail and trend-savvy style confidence that Mac had in spades. But still: Ruby wanted her help as an *assistant*.

"Um, one question: *Why* would I want to work for you?" Mac asked, genuinely curious as to Ruby's twisted logic.

Ruby smiled, looking relieved at the question. She took a deep breath, as though she'd rehearsed what she was about to say. She waited a beat, and then she spoke. "At the ExtravaBAMSa, in my finale speech, I'll tell everyone the video was a fake, a joke that you were in on, and to look for more funny videos at my website.

I'll give you a shout-out, we'll smile, and everyone will think we're BFFs."

Mac paused. For a brief, painful second, she imagined being bossed around by Ruby, or being seen publicly as an assistant, but then she realized that just *thinking about herself* that way was demeaning, and she shook her head. "Very tempting," Mac said sarcastically.

Ruby leaned in so Mac could smell her Christian Lacroix rouge. "Be smart, Mac. I'll let you help out with social chair. And I'll make sure BAMS doesn't hate you like they do now."

"Why should I believe you?"

"What other choice do you have?" Ruby asked seriously.

Mac pressed her Chanel-glossed lips together in a thin line. First of all, Ruby didn't have *that* much power at BAMS. Mac was sure the I.C. downfall had been her own fault. Secondly, Mac never allowed her reputation to be controlled by other people—and certainly *not* by Ruby Goldman. To demean herself by working for Ruby would be too humiliating and unbearable, even if it could (but it couldn't!) mean her comeback.

"Let me think." Mac paused for a second, twisting her Mintee bracelet. "Um, no."

Ruby sighed. "Fine," she said nonchalantly. "Figured I'd throw you a bone. Don't say I didn't try." Ruby popped on her Mac-alike Gucci aviators and headed back to her Hummer. Mac thought she saw a flicker of worry on Ruby's face as she hobbled off.

She closed her front door and made a mental note to donate all seven pairs of her Gucci sunglasses to Goodwill.

Mac had just wandered into the kitchen when her mother barreled in, dropping a pile of scripts with the Initiative logo onto the Sicilian-tiled island.

"What happened today?" Adrienne asked, slowly cocking an eyebrow at Mac. She stared at Mac in a way that meant she knew something was up. Mac felt sick to her stomach, realizing she'd also disappointed her mother in the Slumbergate disaster. "This morning Elliot's assistant canceled our meeting. And then he didn't return my phone call." Adrienne glanced down at her BlackBerry. "We're now going on seven hours and twenty-three minutes of radio silence." No one in Hollywood waited hours, *plural,* to return a call from Adrienne Little-Armstrong. Not even Elliot Tachman.

Unless there was drama. Big Drama.

Just then Maude bounded into the kitchen, her fluffy golden curls bouncing, and taped a new Chess Champion certificate onto the cream-colored Sub-Zero refrigerator, next to last week's Chess Champion certificate. "I won today, Mommy!" Maude exclaimed, pointing at her new prize. Mac rolled her eyes. Why did she always feel like a no-talent loser around her family?

Adrienne leaned down to kiss her youngest child on the forehead. "Wonderful, Maudey! Your sister and I are having a private conversation and I want you to tell me all about this after we're done, okay?" Maude nodded once and immediately walked down the hallway to Adrienne's office. She looked like an adorable little robot.

Adrienne turned to Mac, waiting for an explanation. "Well?"

Mac took a deep breath. "We kind of made fun of Kimmie, but not exactly—Ruby Goldman made it look that way because she taped our iChat conversation, stalker style. Anyway, that's probably why E-Tach called off the meeting. And now everyone at BAMS sort of hates us, too, 'cause we said some mean stuff. Ruby's giving us a chance to redeem ourselves, but it's humiliating, and I'm not lowering myself for anyone," Mac said in a rush.

Adrienne's eyes narrowed, and she became very quiet in a way that Mac knew meant that she was upset. "Are you finished?"

"Yep, I'm ruined." Mac lowered her voice. "And Emily's just destroyed."

"No, I meant, are you finished with this pity party?"

"Mah-um!" Mac said, pushing up the sleeves of her Ron Herman cardigan. "Be serious!" She had expected something along the lines of how pathetic Ruby was. Something that would actually make her feel better.

"I am being serious," Adrienne said, cleaning her Tina Fey glasses on her Vince cashmere sweater. "Would you have said these things about these kids to their faces?

"It was a private conversation!" Mac huffed.

"Mackenzie, I always assume people are recording my conversations." Adrienne put on her glasses.

"But you're an agent!" Mac cried defensively.

"And that's what you want to be, right?" Adrienne pointed out. "Always assume that everything you do on a computer could be viewed by the whole world." Adrienne pulled out a very Post-it-noted script that she had to read for Davey Woodward. "I hate to break it to you, but that was just stupid, hon. Let this be a lesson to you."

"A what?" Mac screeched. She hated the word *lesson* as much as she hated the word *curfew.*

Whose side was she on?

As if reading her mind, Adrienne sighed. "You've been the queen bee your whole life. Maybe now you won't take everyone's respect for granted." She reached into her Birkin bag and pulled out a call sheet, which was a list of the two hundred people whose phone calls she had to return.

Mac's jaw dropped. "Are you seriously saying that I should *humiliate myself*?"

"Look . . ." Adrienne glanced down at the long list of names and phone numbers, scribbling on them with her silver Tiffany pen. "Obviously Ruby's very hurt, and she wants to know that you respect her. This town is all about treating people with respect."

"But Mom!" Mac exclaimed. She took a deep breath to take her voice down a notch, because she knew her mom had a zero-tolerance whining policy. "You would never allow yourself to be disrespected in public!"

"Are you kidding me?" Adrienne put a hand on her Armani-draped hip. "Do you think I just showed up at Initiative and they rolled out the red carpet and said, 'Welcome to the biggest agency in Los Angeles, please be a partner'?"

Mac shook her head, but Adrienne was already on a roll, like an army vet having wartime flashbacks. "Do you know how many months I spent pushing a mail cart before I had the *privilege* of answering people's phones?" Adrienne waved her pen passionately. "Or how many peanut butter shakes I had to order before I had the *great honor* of attending a staff meeting? Or how many years it took me before I got my own e-mail address with my own name? Every day I had to order a chicken salad and then *take the chicken* out of the chicken salad!" Adrienne sighed and leaned closer to Mac, lowering her voice. "I even had to change my name because my boss, *Adrian*, didn't like that he had the same name as a girl. So everyone in the company had to call me *Audrey*!"

Mac laughed despite herself. Her mother would never agree to something like that now. "But I don't want to kiss Ruby's butt just 'cause she's social chair,"

Mac said, staring seriously into her mother's steely blue eyes.

"I'm not saying you kiss her butt—and don't talk like that, it's trashy." Adrienne flicked a crumb off her sweater. "I'm saying you show respect instead of expecting the world to kiss *your* butt, as you so eloquently put it."

Just then Adrienne's cell phone buzzed. She picked it up excitedly. "Bleh. Clooney," she groaned. "When is Elliot going to get over it and stop ignoring me?" She took a deep breath and then snapped into her *I'm so happy to hear from you* voice as she popped the phone to her ear: "Talk to me, Gorgeous!"

Mac waited until her mother had gone down the hallway to her office before she picked up her own phone. Ruby's number was still in her call log. She typed a text as quickly as she could before she changed her mind:

OK YOU'VE GOT A DEAL

Ruby's response came seconds later.

GR8. LET'S DISCUSS. . . . HAVE A FEW OTHER POINTS

Mac cringed, feeling like this story was not about to end well. She took a deep breath and dialed Ruby, remembering she had nowhere to go but up.

CHAPTER TWELVE

COCO

◀ Thursday September 10 ▶

8 AM	Begin life as loser
12:15 PM	Meet at or-gard
3 PM	Get out of BAMS!
4:30 PM	Dance class at the Edge

Coco walked briskly on the dirt path leading to the BAMS organic garden, better known as End of the World. It was at the farthest corner of the school, past the tennis courts, past the eighteenth hole of the golf course, and past the teachers' parking lot. It reeked of compost and alterna-kids. Cell phones didn't even work there. It was like being in Tijuana, which was why Mac's Wednesday night text to meet there had been such a mystery.

Not that Coco wanted to be in a high-traffic zone. She'd already been humiliated twice that day: first when she'd arrived at school and found a giant diaper Scotch-taped to her locker. Then, when she arrived in homeroom, she'd found a handwritten note on her desk that said, *Coco, I Depends on You* atop of a fresh box of Depends. Both times she had calmly dumped the offending material in the trash and pretended like it never happened. And like she couldn't hear the cackles of laughter from people she'd previously considered her friends. But she was on a steady diet of pretending, and it was starting to make her sick.

Coco literally felt nauseated. She hoped it was just the smell of compost.

She trudged onto the dirt path, hoping she didn't get any soil on her pastel pink Luella skirt or crisp white blouse. She tiptoed around tomato plants and cilantro beds until she arrived at the avocado tree where Mac, Becks, and Emily were already waiting. Becks had dark circles under her eyes, and Emily's face was puffy, like she'd been crying. Only Mac looked oddly alert, like she was in an alterna-universe where they still had lives.

Mac stood in front of the avocado tree, wearing a yellow and white Loeffler Randall cotton canvas dress. The girls gathered in a semicircle around her, listening devotedly.

"Good news, girls. I've got a plan," Mac said, clasping her hands together. Her wooden bangles clacked against each other. "I call it 'Pax Rubana.'"

Coco arched a perfectly plucked eyebrow. She wanted to believe this was her first double shot of hope in a very hope-free day. Then again, she'd known Mac long enough to be wary of any Mac schemes that had names. Seventh grade's Mission Meet Suri Cruise and Take Public Transportation to Palm Desert came to mind.

"I did some peacekeeping with Ruby yesterday, and

we worked out a deal," Mac explained. "Basically, we help Ruby, and then she helps us." Mac smiled proudly.

"That's so great!" Emily said, her brown eyes widening.

Coco sighed for Emily's naïveté. She'd been friends with Mac long enough to know that Mac could spin better than DJ Aoki. "Okay, so what's the pitch?" Coco put her arm on her hip and twirled the Inner Circle ring that dangled from her neck.

"It's very easy." Mac looked down at the dirt and inhaled. And then, like a roller-coaster ride at Magic Mountain, she let her words free-fall: "Becks-you-train-Ellie-Parker-to-surf-Ems-you-help-Kimmie-and-Coco-you're-the-water-boy-for-the-dance-team-Basically-we're-all-just-assistants-for-two-weeks-And-that's-it-It-will-be-easy-and-maybe-even-fun."

But Coco had heard everything. And she was totally over hiding her true feelings. "Is this a *joke*?" she cried. "Are you for serious? Did you just say *water boy*? The only *Waterboy* I know is an Adam Sandler movie from like a million years ago that I didn't see," Coco said. Once people saw you as the water-fetcher, they would never see you as a dancer. She glanced at Becks, double-checking that they were both *not* on board.

"No way, dude!" Becks said, shaking her head vigorously. She pulled down the sleeves of her sweatshirt so it looked like she had no hands. "I'm not helping Ellie!"

Emily looked down at the ground, making the letter *E*

in the dirt with her checkerboard Vans. She looked like she was ready to cry, and Coco thought she heard a sniffle. She felt bad for Ems, who was so far from home. Bel-Air was hard enough when you were *from* here.

Mac looked down at the tomato plant, as though it could tell her how to convince her friends. Finally she said, "It's not like I'm asking you to do things I wouldn't do."

"Then what do *you* have to do?" Coco asked, crossing her arms over her chest. She couldn't imagine Mac stooping to any fate as low as water boy.

Mac clenched her teeth: "I'm Ruby's assistant."

Coco and Becks laughed. Mac working as anyone's assistant, let alone Ruby's, was not something that could happen in her lifetime—it was as likely as Jessica Simpson winning an Oscar.

"Wait, Mac!" Coco warned, her tone suddenly serious: "She's Barry Goldman's daughter. Are you insane?" Ruby's father was notorious for being one of the most cold-blooded bosses in town.

"He fired some kid on Pacific Coast Highway and made him walk home carrying a flat-screen TV. For twenty miles," Becks said, shaking her head in horror.

"He threw a stapler at his assistant," Coco added in a fierce whisper. "That assistant now has a staple permanently embedded in his eyebrow."

Emily looked frozen in horror.

"You guys, please!" Mac begged, smoothing her

dress. "It's only for nine days, until ExtravaBAMSa blows over. And I'm not working for Barry. I'm working for *Ruby*. Remember: We insulted the entire school. They think we're all conceited snobs," Mac said, the closest she'd come to pleading. "So now we humble ourselves and show respect."

"I don't see what that does except embarrass us." Becks shrugged.

"Girls, if we meet her demands, Ruby is going to tell everyone that the video was just a big joke. And if we *don't*, then she is *never* going to let BAMS forget about this. And besides, it's only for, like, nine days."

And that was nine days too many.

"Mac Little-A, I love you, but no." Coco looked down at her D&G watch. "I gotta go. I still have to dance today." She had signed up for private classes at the Edge Studio since quitting the team. It wasn't quite the same as being the elected captain of the Bam-Bams, but it was a start.

"Yeah, and I just gotta go," Becks muttered, not even bothering to say why. Emily looked back and forth between Mac and the other girls. Then she mouthed, "Sorry," to Coco and Becks and stood by Mac, who was staring at Coco and Becks in disbelief.

Coco grabbed Becks's hand and they stepped over a flower bed and back onto the dirt. When they had reached the end of the garden, almost back into the working cell-phone zone, they spotted the wannabe-goth twins, Jaden and Slate Shean, sitting on the white picket fence blocking their exit. They were wearing black skinny jeans and black pseudo-vintage Ramones T-shirts. The brothers Shean were frail, pale, and generally annoying to girls. They thought they were so out there because they wore all black (even though they shopped at Urban Outfitters) and had weird bowl haircuts. Really they were just Pete Wentz, minus the music talent and famous wife.

"Hey, Becks!" said Jaden. "Want some Pinkberry?" He pantomimed licking frozen yogurt. His tongue looked freakishly long.

"We got extra!" yelled Slate. Or was it Jaden? Coco could never tell them apart. She squeezed Becks's arm and accidentally stepped on an overripe Japanese eggplant. It squirted something gross on her Tory Burch ballet flat.

"Coco, maybe you can fertilize it!" the other twin yelled. They high-fived like it was the greatest thing ever in their not-really-alterna-lives. Then, spotting Emily, they made cat paws with their pale hands.

"Go apply eyeliner!" Emily screamed from behind them, shocking both Becks and Coco.

If the Shean twins were mocking her, then Coco had hit rock bottom ages ago and was now somewhere near China. Mac was right: She really didn't have any other options—she had to make this situation better soon.

Coco grabbed Becks's hand and stormed back to Mac. "I can't take this anymore. I'm in!"

"I guess I am too," Becks said glumly, tying the strings on her sweatshirt.

"Ditto," Emily said shyly.

"Nice!" Mac smiled. "Trust me—this will be a cake-walk!" She sounded confident, but Coco knew her friend's turquoise eyes were hiding anxiety.

Coco imagined fetching water for her friends while they danced. But it was only for a short time, and it would get her back on the team. "Okay, if I'm gonna go be water girl, then I gotta bounce!" She blew an air kiss at the group and raced off.

She was about to walk toward school, but then, spotting the twins perched on the white picket fence like alterna–guard dogs, Coco thought better of it and walked all the way to the back of the field to take the south exit, just to avoid the Shean brothers.

Twelve minutes later, and totally out of breath, Coco darted into the dance studio, which was almost as big as her private studio. There were gold-framed pictures of the Bam-Bams, a surround-sound system, and shiny wood floors. The room smelled like sweat and pine wood cleaner with a hint of lavender room spray. Haylie was leading the group in stretching at the bars, which lined the mirrored walls.

"What are you doing here?" Haylie asked, standing

on her right leg, her left leg balanced over the bar. She wore a purple leotard and purple American Apparel shorts and way too much makeup for a practice (lip shimmer, eyeliner, mascara, and blush). The other girls, who were stretching on the bar behind Haylie, turned and faced Coco, like an army of one-legged robots. They looked like a Capezioed centipede.

"I'm the water boy." Coco forced a smile, her cheeks burning. Coco was never good at faking her feelings: She was as see-through as chiffon.

The other Bam-Bams looked surprised. Near the front of the ballet bar, Lucia leaned in to face Maribel and they giggled. Coco stiffened, wondering why so many smart girls (who, up until Wednesday, had been her friends) had turned against her so easily. What made even less sense was how they could so blindly follow Haylie "Seven-Second Delay" Fowler, who was the only person who *didn't* seem surprised by Coco's odd grand entrance. Ruby had obviously filled Haylie in on the plan already.

"Glad to have you here," Haylie said, as though she and Coco were total strangers meeting for the first time. "Water's over there." She pointed toward a giant cardboard box of Fiji waters in the far corner of the studio. "The bottles should really be in a pyramid formation." She went back to stretching.

Coco stepped out of her muddy, eggplant-stained flats and dragged her feet over to the corner of the studio to begin her first task. She settled down on the glossy blond wood floor and started stacking Fiji bottles one by one. The girls moved away from the bar, toward the middle of the studio.

It was quiet in the studio. Peaceful, even. At least no one could make fun of her here. And at least she'd get her place back eventually. *Maybe this wasn't so bad?*

"Umbrella" started playing over the sound system, and Coco's heart thumped sadly as she watched the girls take their first position and hit their steps—*her steps*. Maribel bumped into Taylor and they all had a giggle break while the song played. They looked like they were having so much fun.

Coco forced her gaze away from her ex-teammates and back to her water bottle pyramid-in-progress. It was bad enough to be made fun of by the entire school, and it was even worse to have to be the water boy, but to have to miss dancing her own routine . . . That hurt most of all.

CHAPTER THIRTEEN

becks

◀ Thursday September 10 ▶

2:55 PM School's out

4:15 PM Meet Ellie for TBL (Torture Becks Lesson) #1

WHY WHY WHY WHY

Becks entered the Grove by Morels French steakhouse just as a giant wood-paneled trolley packed with tourists passed. The Grove was like the Disneyland of outdoor malls, which was why it had a trolley and a footbridge and fountains and its own souvenir memorabilia. Becks felt so totally confused and frustrated that she had to stop and sit on a bench because she was staring so intently at her phone. It was official: Becks hated text messages. They were never good news. The last one from Ellie had made no sense:

C U AT THE GROVE @ 415.

In fact, it made *negative* sense. Becks had replied HUH? and assumed Ellie would call to explain that it had all been a typo and she had meant to write CU AT THE BEACH @ 415 and then they would go surfing in Malibu.

But no.

Instead the reply was:

C U @ QUIKSILVER STORE AT 415!

As if the added exclamation point made it make so much more sense. How would meeting at the mall help Ellie learn to surf? And why was Ellie suddenly obsessed with surfing? Becks arrived at Quiksilver at exactly four fifteen, only because she knew the other girls were upholding their ends of Pax Rubana.

Becks scanned the giant store, her eyes moving from the brown stone floor, to the racks of bikinis and windbreakers, to the blown-up pictures of happy athletic models. Becks shivered—she always felt like a fish out of water in stores, even if they sold things she would wear. If Becks had free time, she spent it surfing, not shopping for things she could *wear* surfing.

Then her eyes landed on Ellie, waiting by a row of sandals with a perky smile and a Coffee Bean Iced Blended. She promptly threw away her barely touched drink the second she saw Becks.

"Hey, Becks, way to be on time!" Ellie said. When she wasn't speaking in baby talk, she had a loudmouth voice, and sort of sounded like she was making fun of people.

They stood there while tanned girls passed by in velour sundresses and flip-flops. Becks was so disoriented that she barely noticed Zac Efron exiting the store clutching a huge white shopping bag.

Becks hung her hands in the front pocket of her baby blue Maui & Sons sweatshirt. "So I don't get why I'm here," she said slowly, trying not to sound witchy, since there was no point in making the experience even more brutal.

"I know, it's totally weird," Ellie giggled. It sounded like she said *tolly weir.* "I was going to meet you at the beach and then I was like . . . I can't go surfing!" She paused as if reenacting her lightbulb moment. "I have nuh-thing to wear!" She tugged her white terry-cloth miniskirt so that it hung below her hipbones.

Becks wanted to be a team player for the Inner Circle, but this was *ridiculous*. Sure, she could surf, but what did she know about *shopping*? And then, as if Ellie had ESP, she giggled. "You sooooo don't want to be here right now."

Becks shrugged.

Ellie smiled condescendingly, as if Becks's discomfort was adorable. They walked past the shoes and the sundresses, and Ellie began looking at the racks of miniskirts. She held up a Roxy T-shirt and then, as if remembering she was there for surfing, she giggled and put it back. "For reals, Bexy, I want to look cuuute. I don't want to look like some lame poser! Ugh." She stuck out her tongue.

"Ellie, I can't advise you about clothes." Becks said. She was not about to admit that she e-mailed Mac photos every night of her next day's ensemble. "When I surf, I just wear whatever feels right."

"Don't worry. I know what looks good on me. Duh." Ellie pointed at herself. In addition to the miniskirt, she was wearing a tight white tank top that showed off her C-cups, and cream-colored Ugg boots, even though it was 82 degrees outside. She reached for a shiny metallic bikini.

"I just don't know what's surfer-y and what's not. You need to tell me what are killer surfing clothes." She flashed a bright white smile at Becks, who winced at the word *killer* and the term *surfing clothes* and especially their appearing right next to each other in a sentence, said aloud. But Becks didn't correct Ellie and trailed behind her, glancing around the store, hoping they at least sold surf wax so something productive would come of this trip.

"Why do you want to surf so badly?" Becks asked as they moved toward a rack of tropical-print bikinis.

"I think it's rad that you do," Ellie said, without thinking. In fact, her reply came so quickly that for a second Becks thought she had to be serious.

"Really?" Becks asked. She had always suspected Ellie was just trying to get close to Austin.

"Duh." Ellie shrugged. "Who doesn't think surfing is cool?"

Becks smiled at the backhanded compliment. She imagined how proud Austin would be of her, teaching a newbie to surf.

Soon Ellie had a pile of *surfing clothes*, aka Roxy bikinis, draped over her teensy little arm, and she darted into a dressing room. Becks sat down on one of the royal blue velvet futons that faced the white doors and picked up a copy of *Surfer*. She flipped through images of surfers poking out of monstrous waves, wishing she too were at the beach—or anywhere but the mall.

Ellie emerged in the first of her *surfing outfits* in a lime green and black bikini. "I look like a tool, right?"

Becks laughed at Ellie's self-awareness. At least that was a nice surprise.

"I wouldn't say *tool*," Becks began. "It's just a *lot* of green."

"Done! Adios!" Ellie said, heading back into the changing room.

Next Ellie appeared in a blue and white–trimmed bikini that showed off her flat stomach, ripples of abs, and C-cups. "What do we think?" She spun around, wedgie-checking herself as she turned.

"Um, it's gonna fall off before you get in the water?" Becks warned.

"Uh-oh. We don't want that!" Ellie giggled, heading back into the room.

Becks secretly picked up her iPhone and sent a check-in text to the Inner Circle, telling them she was being Mac for an hour. Really, it wasn't *sooo* bad. She took off her sweatshirt so she was wearing just her favorite eco-friendly T-shirt, which had a picture of Kermit the Frog and said THINK GREEN.

Seconds later, Ellie tried on a plain black bikini, with thicker straps and just a hint of pink in the Roxy logo on her chest. The top looked a little sports bra–esque, but it was the kind of suit you really could surf in. "Poser girl or surfer girl?" Ellie asked, her hands on her hips as she glimpsed herself dubiously in the three-way mirror.

Becks put down her phone. She was stunned. Ellie didn't just look like a surfer girl. She looked like someone Becks would go surfing *with*. Becks almost wanted to say *poser* just because she didn't want to help a Rubybot in any way, but then she realized: It was kind of fun to help Ellie. Who knew Becks could pick out clothes without Mac?

"Surfer. Totes," Becks said, her leg dangling over the futon. And then, as a joke, she yelled, "Cowabunga, brah!" She shook her hand hang-loose style, with her thumb and pinky sticking out. It was the ultimate poser move.

And then, from behind them, a man's voice called: "Cowabunga is right! Lookin' good!" Becks turned around and saw a man nodding at Ellie. He had sun-streaked hair and he was about six-foot two, wearing a long-sleeved yellow tee that said QUIKSILVER on the sleeves, and faded army-print cargo shorts. He was tanned, and he had crinkles around his eyes like an ex-surfer.

Becks and Ellie made insta–eye contact. They weren't BFFs, but this guy seemed like a perv.

"Dude! Not trying to be skeevy." He put his hands up in surrender. "I get how this looks. I'm Chad. Chad

Hutchins. I work for Quiksilver." He waved, and Becks winced that she'd just said *Cowabunga* and *brah* in the presence of someone who (1) knew how ridiculous that sounded and (2) clearly *did not* know she was kidding. She wanted to explain that it had been an *ironic* use of the phrase. Chad put two business cards on the glass side table by Becks. "I'm a recruiter for our girls' team." He nodded at Ellie. "So you're a surfer?" Chad asked.

Ellie nodded and giggled.

Becks's jaw dropped. Was Ellie for serious?

"Great, 'cause we're always looking to sponsor new talent." Chad nodded his head as he spoke. "And for models for some of our new lines."

"Great, 'cause I'd love to get sponsored!" Ellie said enthusiastically. Becks shot her a dagger glare. How could she get *sponsored* when she didn't know how to *surf*? And how could she not at least *mention* that Becks was the star surfer at BAMS? All Becks wanted was a little backup. Becks imagined Ellie getting sponsored by Roxy or Quiksilver and getting sent to Hawaii for one of their sponsored events, and getting all their new bikinis and wet suits sent to her for free, all because she pretended to be a surfer. Becks's nostrils flared angrily that Ellie wasn't going to at least mention that Becks was the real surfer. Then she remembered: Ellie was not her friend.

"I surf too," Becks said, trying to sound casual and not at all like a Big Scary Freak (BSF) about it. Becks had never really thought about modeling before, but she didn't want to see Ellie get an opportunity that should be hers.

Chad spun around. "Right on, brah! Cowabunga!"

Becks covered her mouth in surprise, realizing he thought *she* was the lame friend.

Chad turned to face Ellie again. In her black bikini, with her tan, toned arms, Ellie looked a thousand times more surfer than Becks, who was wearing a Think Green tee and jeans. "If you ever want us to come to one of your competitions, give a call, okay?" He made a little phone signal with his hand. "I'm serious. You call me."

"Great, Serious, I'm Ellie. I'll call ya." She winked. "If you're lucky." She reached over to the glass table to grab a business card, then darted back into her changing room, leaving Becks and Chad all alone.

Becks felt desperate to say something, anything, but she felt like she was underwater and didn't know how to get the words out. Chad had already decided which BAMS girl was the surfer, and that was Ellie. Becks had that same jealous/left-out/I'm-invisible feeling she'd had when Ellie and Austin flirted uncontrollably at the beach in front of her. Both times she'd felt like Ellie was sweeping in and stealing what belonged to her. Her head was pounding.

"Laters!" Chad said to Ellie's retreating back. Then he looked at Becks. "Take care, buddy." He mimed punching the air and strolled out. The second he left the store's granite floor, Becks whispered, "I've surfed the Pipeline." But it was too late. No one heard.

Numbly Becks took Chad's other card and put it into her jeans pocket, wishing she'd not been such a BSF. What could she even say if she called him? *Hi, I'm the mute who said nothing when you introduced yourself at the Grove? I think I'd be a great spokesgirl despite the fact that I did not actually speak?*

"Why were you so quiet back there?" Ellie asked, sauntering out of the changing room in her miniskirt and Uggs, the bikinis draped over her arm. She looked genuinely confused.

"You should have said something," Ellie continued. "You're, like, the best surfer ever. Duh." She strolled over to the cashier at the front of the store, leaving Becks to follow her like a total tool. Ellie plopped her things on the cashier's countertop, popping some Dentyne Ice while the cashier began ringing up the clothes.

Becks flinched: Ellie was right. No one had forced her to be a mute freak. She robotically put her hands on the counter, trying to forget how she'd just wiped out an opportunity. It was like Ellie had just ridden a killer wave while Becks had watched from the shore.

Ellie turned to Becks excitedly, trying on a pair of Roxy sunglasses. "Pretty sweet, huh?" Ellie said, tugging her miniskirt, but it sounded like *preh-ee swee.* "You know who else is going to want to hear from me when you teach me to surf?" Ellie fanned herself with Chad's business card. She was smiling and staring at Becks. "Austin."

Becks jerked back at hearing the name Austin, which hit her like a gush of salt water up the nose. She stood straight up and rigid, her eyes wide as she stared coldly at Ellie. She had tried to give Ellie the benefit of the doubt, she had tried to believe that Ellie was really doing this for the love of the sport, but now here was proof that Ellie was only doing this to get Austin's attention.

Ellie reached into her silver Marc Jacobs wallet to grab her American Express Platinum card, totally unaware of the storm brewing inside Becks.

Becks clenched her teeth, sulking too much to say anything. She had agreed to teach Ellie to surf. She had not agreed to watch Ellie steal her dreams.

CHAPTER FOURTEEN

emily

◀ Thursday September 10 ▶

4:30 PM Meet Kimmie to find out my task—eek!

AT SOME POINT TODAY: Still need to figure out where everything at BAMS is

Emily sat on one of the mahogany leather benches in the BAMS auditorium, checking the weather in Cedartown (64 degrees) on her iPhone, waiting for Kimmie Tachman. They hadn't spoken since Slumbergate. Emily wanted to explain to Kimmie, *I like you! I really do!* But it seemed silly: Actions (for example, cat paw impressions) that were caught on camera and e-mailed to the entire school spoke much louder than words.

A text from Becks to the Inner Circle popped up on her phone:

I'M BEING MAC TODAY. BEEN @ GROVE FOR AN HR

Mac's response came almost instantly: DO IT 4 THE IC!!!

Emily cringed for Becks, knowing that for her, mall time equaled jail time.

Coco's was next: B GLAD U DON'T HAVE 2 MAKE WTR BTLE PYRAMIDS!!!

Emily started to add her own Mac-style pep-text to

the mix, when Kimmie bounded in, wearing Joe's jeans with a pink necktie as a belt, and a fuchsia hoodie. For a second, Emily thought that Kimmie actually looked cute. Then Kimmie turned and Emily realized that the hoodie said FLIRT in girly, sequined script on the back.

"Hi, Emily!" Kimmie said cheerfully, as though Slumbergate had never happened.

Emily smiled, relieved that Kimmie wasn't going to be mean to her. "Look, I just want to say that I'm sorry," Emily said gingerly, rubbing her hands on her yellow Diesel jeans. "There was more that night—"

"Look, I haaaate to get caught up in all this drama," Kimmie interrupted, waving a hand. She sat down on the bench and put an arm around Emily like they were BFFs. "Plus, let's face it: The enemies you make on the way up are the ones you see on the way down. My dad says that *all the time*. I am so not looking for enemies."

"Me neither," Emily said, feeling relieved.

"Good-we-agree-on-that," Kimmie said. But she wasn't listening. She was rifling through the oversize white Coach bag by her feet. "Ta-da!" she said, pulling out a thin packet of paper with a brass brad in the far-left corner. She handed it delicately to Emily, like it was a glass slipper.

Emily looked at the stack of papers anxiously. She gulped, hoping it wasn't a list of everything she'd have to do for Kimmie.

"It's my one-act play!" Kimmie exclaimed. "It's called *Judgers and Haters*."

Emily blinked. *This* was her punishment? To *act* in a play?

"It's my baby," Kimmie said, hugging the script to her pink-clad chest. "And you're the star. You're the only one I trust to play the lead."

Emily looked down at the script excitedly. "What's it about?" she asked, her mind buzzing. Her punishment was to embrace her newfound passion? To do the one thing she'd moved to Los Angeles to do? It was what she would have chosen for herself.

Kimmie smiled proudly. "It's about this girl who lives alone in a cabin and she is a total judger and hater, but the reason she's that way is 'cause that's how the world treats her. Everyone think she's a loser." Kimmie made an *L* with her thumb and index finger and brought it to her forehead. "And so one day this cute girl from Bel-Air knocks at her door and the loser girl kidnaps the cute Bel-Air girl and locks her in the cabin. And at the end of the two-woman show they understand each other better and the loser girl brings down the house with a really powerful monologue confronting stereotypes. It's a comedy-slash-thriller."

Emily considered the role. It seemed like something she could handle. Sure, it wouldn't be super exciting to play a cute Bel-Air girl trapped in a cabin, but at least it meant that Kimmie thought she was fitting in.

"So you're going to play the role of the loser," Kimmie continued. "Spazmo! It's sooooo fun for the actor—I mean, *you*! 'Cause no one knows if he / she / it is a guy or a girl."

Emily tried to swallow but her throat was clamping. Spazmo? A loser *and* androgynous?

"You'll need to use a really deep voice, which we know you can do, *Tom*," Kimmie said in an accusatory tone. Emily winced at the memory of the last time she played a guy. She remembered telling Mac specifically she was too new to make enemies, and now here was proof she'd been right.

Kimmie reached into her never-ending Coach torture sack and pulled out Charlie Chaplin glasses and a huge red flannel hat that looked like it belonged on a man who hunted and never showered. "For your character."

Emily opened the heavy black frames, the worst look for her pale face, and held them like they were a ticking time bomb. She imagined herself acting like a freaky girl / guy in the world's ugliest outfit. Ew. Not even Jessica Alba could look good in that.

Her mind was racing for ways to get out of this politely. Remembering Adrienne's advice, she knew she had to stay *adored*. "Don't you want to hold auditions?" Emily asked meekly. "Gosh, I'd hate to take such a great role if I don't deserve it."

"No need." Kimmie waved away the idea. She

looked seriously at Emily. "I only want to work with people I admire."

"Yeah, but you never know," Emily squeaked. "Or maybe you should take this, since you know it so well?"

"Well, actually, I *was* going to play the role myself." Kimmie paused, as if remembering something. "But then I changed my mind."

Emily stared at Kimmie curiously, wondering if there was more to this story.

"But I am taking the supporting role in this. I play the cute, all-American girl next-door, Kipleigh, who wanders into Spazmo's lonely life and shows her that there's no reason to hate the whole world." Kimmie shrugged and pushed up the sleeves of her fuchsia hoodie. "Besides, I need to save my energy for directing."

"So we'll be acting together?" Emily asked, faking enthusiasm.

But Kimmie was on a roll and not listening. "You should probably Netflix *Boys Don't Cry* to get a sense of this part." She stared at Emily, her tiny brown eyes crinkling in concentration. "Spazmo should definitely be a freak. I want people to leave the play feeling awful for you."

Emily nodded numbly. She realized the get-out-of-playing-Spazmo train had already left the station. Was Kimmie trying to torture her? Or did she really want the best actress to be in her play? Or both? She picked up the glasses and held them in front of her face to inspect them, mentally calculating how many people would see her as Spazmo. At least it was just a school play. No one would see it.

"Oooh! I almost forgot—this is your headgear!" Kimmie waved it in the air like a pompon. "It used be mine, so you know it's real." She grinned. "Don't worry, I totally sterilized it in the dishwasher."

Emily nodded, eyeing the metal device. It reminded her of going to the dentist.

"Put the costume on! Let's run some lines!" Kimmie clapped enthusiastically.

Emily put on the glasses and the flannel and opened to page one of the script. She inhaled and then uttered her first line, fearfully, like she was jumping off the high dive. "Knock, knock—who's at my door?" Emily-as-Spazmo read her line. To her surprise, for a second she felt joy at rehearsing, something she hadn't done since prepping for her audition with Mac.

"That's great, but can you add a lisp?" Kimmie asked sweetly.

"Knock, knock—whoth at my door?" Emily added obediently.

"Great, and just be a little bit more monster-y?" Kimmie suggested.

Emily read the line again, this time with an even deeper, louder voice and with her shoulders hunched up so high they practically touched her ears. She felt like a troll.

As they continued to run lines, Emily starting getting into the part, and line after line made both girls chuckle. Emily wasn't sure if it was because she sounded like such a freak or because the play was actually funny. But at least for a second she made herself laugh.

"Oh my gosh, I almost forgot!" Kimmie crossed her arms and stared at Emily. It was almost like an accusation. "I insist on method acting!"

Emily gulped. Method acting meant totally immersing yourself in a role, and it meant a lot of different things to different people. Some actors behaved like they were in character *all the time*. Emily's mind raced, imagining what Kimmie could mean by "method." She knew Dustin Hoffman had once gone two days without sleeping in order to tap into his character for *Marathon Man*. Emily didn't want to give Kimmie any ideas. "What exactly do you mean by *method acting*?" Emily said cautiously.

"Like, you know how you tricked me at the Grove and made me think you were a guy? Nice job, by the way." Kimmie redid her ponytail and Emily wondered just how much bitterness Kimmie was storing. Maybe she wasn't so sweet after all? "I want you to immerse yourself in this role twenty-four-seven."

"So what you're saying is, I need to be Spazmo *all the time*?" Emily spoke slowly, hoping she'd missed something. Emily imagined walking through Main Quad dressed like Spazmo, walking into classes dressed like

Spazmo, searching for her lunch table like Spazmo, and feeling everyone's eyes on her as Spazmo. She was so new at BAMS that no one really knew who she was. If she had to method-act for Spazmo, then everyone would think she really *was* a total freak. Surely Kimmie wasn't *that* cruel.

"Yes, starting now." Kimmie smiled.

Emily felt trapped—she wondered what Adrienne would say. But of course she couldn't bother Adrienne with something this petty. Plus, she knew Mac and the Inner Circle were counting on her to do her part. If any one of them didn't fulfill their part of Pax Rubana, the whole deal was shot. Emily had no choice.

Emily opened her mouth to speak. She was about to say, "But nobody at BAMS knows me yet and they're going to think I really *am* Spazmo!" But then she looked into Kimmie's twinkling eyes and realized: *That was exactly the point.*

CHAPTER FIFTEEN

mac

◀ Thursday September 10 ▶

3:30 PM Pre–Pax Rubana Chocolate pedicure @ Bliss

5:15 PM Go be Ruby's (gulp) asst (I refuse to type that entire word)

8:30 PM Post–Pax Rubana bubble bath—L'Occitane bath salts, *je t'adore!*

Mac inhaled deeply as Erin's Prius wound up the tree-lined streets of Benedict Canyon and then turned right onto Mulholland Drive, passing Spanish-style homes hidden behind black gates, and tourists stopping on the side of the road to take pictures. From her seat in the Prius, Mac had a crystal-clear view of the Valley to her left, and the Beverly Hills canyons to the right.

Erin turned the car into a private driveway with a guardhouse, where Ruby lived in a private gated community called Beverly Park. Everyone called it Beverly Barf, because of its ten-bedroom nouveau riche houses. Davey Woodward had moved his extended family into one of those huge houses when he became a millionaire movie star. Erin gave her name to the guard, who let them in.

"So . . . are you friends with Ruby Goldman?" Erin asked, her green eyes bugging behind her red Ugly Betty glasses as they drove down the private road. It was dotted with matching, ginormous Italian villas with ornate fountains and tennis courts and sprawling lawns. "Is she as bad as her father?" Erin whispered cautiously, as if Barry Goldman might overhear. "I had a friend who worked for him, and he got fired for buying the wrong flavor soy milk."

"Actually, I'm Ruby's assistant." Mac slipped on her new Balenciaga wraparound sunglasses, trying to hide her disdain for the *A*-word, since she didn't want to offend Erin.

"How is Mac Little-Armstrong anyone's *assistant*?" Erin said incredulously, her silver nose ring shining in the sunlight.

"It's a long story." Mac shrugged. "A long, humiliating story involving my big mouth that ends with me being an assistant."

"Well, now we have something in common!" Erin squealed, hitting the Prius steering wheel overexcitedly with her overly ringed hands. She accidentally honked the horn. Erin was living proof that not everyone outgrew their awkward years. "No offense, but Ruby's dad makes the worst movies," Erin continued. "They're like car chases and explosions with bad dialogue and fake cleavage."

Mac smiled, pleased that even someone as clueless as Erin knew that Ruby came from tacky stock. It was true: Ruby's dad directed big-budget action movies that were jam-packed with explosions and bad dialogue. But they were always blockbusters, which was why he was very rich and powerful.

When they arrived at 519 Beverly Park Road, Mac gulped at the sight of Ruby's sun-yellow Italian villa. Like the other houses in Beverly Park, the Goldman residence was ostentatiously beautiful, but it was shielded by spiky iron gates, fences, and barbed wire. It looked like a prison.

Erin stopped the silver Prius in front of a gate with a giant gold *G* the size of a small child and buzzed the intercom. Seconds later, the gate opened ominously, like a drawbridge. Mac felt like she was on her way to medieval torture. All they needed was a moat.

"I wonder how much it costs to have an electric gate?" Erin asked cheerfully. Mac turned to face Erin, noticing her bright red lipstick and bright white teeth, and for the first time ever Mac realized why she was so nonstop talky: She drove around all day running errands. She was lonely.

Because being a personal assistant was the worst job in the world.

Ruby's maid answered the doorbell, wearing a formal black and white maid's outfit. Either she didn't speak much English or she didn't want to. She pointed at a long corridor.

Mac walked down the hallway, passing an indoor

swimming pool, a bowling alley, and a private Pilates studio with a Reformer machine. With every step Mac took on the marble floors, she realized that the Goldman house felt un-lived-in, like a museum, but borderline scary. There was almost no furniture, but there were oil paintings everywhere. Supposedly Barry Goldman was a huge modern art fan, but Mac thought his paintings were just weird. One was an orange triangle with a blue circle inside. Another was just a splotch of red on white canvas, like a drop of blood.

The long hallway led to a spiral staircase, with curved walls that were like a photo-shrine to Ruby. Mac crept up the stairs, eyeing the pictures of Ruby in small black frames. They'd all been taken within the past year, after Ruby's summer weight loss. (Did her family not think she was worth photographing before?) Mac spotted a picture of Ruby with Drew Barrymore. She took another step. There was Ruby smiling with Jessica Biel. Ruby with Shia La Beouf. Ruby with Britney. In all, there were forty-nine pictures of Ruby with famous people. (Pictures of Ruby with friends: zero).

Finally Mac reached the top of the staircase and stood in front of a white door with giant red-block letters that spelled RUBY. Huffing and puffing, Mac made a mental note to take more Burn 60 classes in Brentwood to get in shape. She knocked twice.

"Come in!" Ruby cooed.

Mac slowly pushed open the door. The bedroom

smelled like it had been misted in Tocca room freshener, and Christina Aguilera's "Ain't No Other Man" was playing from Ruby's MacBook computer.

"Welcome!" Ruby called. She was lying on the custard-colored bedspread of her canopy-covered bed, her feet and head propped up by a mountain of white lace pillows. Her crutches were leaning against her white nightstand. Ruby wore a pewter Graham & Spencer dress with silver-trimmed sneakers. Mac winced, knowing that she had debuted that dress last spring. Ruby had no doubt copied her, because Ruby copied everything Mac wore.

Ruby's bedroom was painted cream and had frilly lace curtains on all the French windows, and cream-colored Anthropologie furniture. It was almost grandma-chic, Mac decided, until she looked up behind Ruby's bed and noticed a life-size oil portrait of Ruby sitting on a white horse. The room was officially downgraded to Tackorama status. Mac made a mental note to tell the I.C.

"Hi, Macdaddy!" Ruby said sweetly.

"Don't call me that," Mac said calmly, stepping closer to Ruby's bed.

"Whatever, Trevor." Ruby smiled.

"Bumsies you're on crutches," Mac said, eyeing Ruby's heavily bandaged ankle.

"Yeah, it would be a bummer." Ruby smiled. "Except that it's not."

"But crutches must be really hard on your pop career," Mac fake-sympathized.

"Yeah, except that I still have my contract with Brigs. While I'm hurt, we're just focusing on my singing. In fact, I'm going to sing my ode to BAMS at the ExtravaBAMSa finale." And then, without even pausing to think how awkward it would be to sing in front of just one person, Ruby closed her eyes and sang Gwen Stefani angry-style:

Wham BAMS

Thank you ma'am.

"Ooooh, great," Mac said fake-sweetly. Inside she was totally annoyed that everything was working out for Ruby when things should have been working out for *her*. Not only would Ruby be the speaker at ExtravaBAMSa, but she also had a record deal? It was too obnoxious.

Mac decided to put the brakes on that subject. "What do you want me to do, Rubes?" She pushed up the sleeves on her James Perse tee and stuffed her hands into her Paige jeans. She was not about to dress down just because she was an assistant.

"The first thing I'd like you to do," Ruby cooed, reading from a giant index card, "is organize my closet." She pointed a remote control at the opposite corner of her room and clicked a button. Immediately a shuttered door slid up, like a garage door.

As the door inched its way up, the closet slowly came into view. First Mac saw the floor, which was covered in shoes. Then the door opened a little more, to reveal jeans. Then sweaters. And as it inched up the wall, unveiling a cavern of cotton, Mac realized: The "closet" was more like a separate wing of the house. And it looked like there had been an explosion of clothes: They were everywhere but on hangers.

Mac's jaw dropped, but she quickly recovered and made a stoic face. The last thing she wanted was to seem fazed by anything Ruby had plotted for her. This wasn't exactly how she'd envisioned "assisting Ruby as social chair," Mac realized, as she pulled her hair into a ponytail. Then she imagined her mother making a peanut butter smoothie back when she really wanted to be an agent. She thought of Coco toughing it out as a water boy, Becks having to go shopping with Ellie, and Emily doing whatever it was Kimmie had in store for her. Ugh. *Everybody has to pay their dues,* Mac reminded herself. And at least her dues were being paid in the privacy of Ruby's home.

Mac tiptoed over to the mess, not quite believing she was essentially going to be a maid. Spying the dirty socks on the carpet, she froze, realizing she'd actually have to touch them in order to put them in the hamper.

"Do you mind if I organize everything by color?" Mac asked, surveying the mess. That was how her three closets had been professionally organized by California Closets. They had totally overhauled her wardrobe, leaving behind pristine shelves and a color-coded organizing system. Her closet now rivaled the racks at Planet Blue.

"Fabulous, organize by color." Ruby followed on her crutches while Mac began to make piles of clothing. "Just so you know, I decided to go with Joan's on Third for the ExtravaBAMSa buffet." She gave Mac a *what do you think?* look.

"Nice," Mac said, impressed. It *was* a good choice. Joan's on Third had crowd-pleasing vegetables and sandwiches, and they were famous for their turkey meat loaf and their cupcakes. The idea of Ruby actually doing a good job as social chair made Mac a little sad.

Ruby smiled. She actually seemed relieved to get Mac's approval. "I'm also going with Sweet Lady Jane for some additional desserts," she said gingerly. "I'm thinking the triple-berry cake."

"Good choice. Make sure you tell them to come early." Mac leaned down to pick up some jeans. "People want to see the dessert when they walk in. It makes for a good impression, even if they don't eat it until much later."

"Okay, and they're good, right?" Ruby asked, tugging at a hangnail on her index finger.

"Of course," Mac said.

And then, as if realizing she was revealing insecurities, Ruby sighed. "I should go meet the caterers. They're waiting for me downstairs. Just thought you'd like to know what was up."

"Yeah, thanks," Mac said, hating that for once in her life she really was jealous of Ruby Goldman. She groaned silently and went back to her mission. She stood on a little white stepladder and grabbed a pair of two-years-ago True Religion jeans from a high shelf. They were in the double-digit size, a remnant of when the brand was cool and Ruby was big. Mac wondered if Ruby kept them as a reminder of her old self, since they'd fit two of her now.

As Mac collected the clothes, she suddenly felt like she was Kate Moss inspecting Sienna Miller's closet. Looking at Ruby's wardrobe was almost like staring at her own. Ruby had ripped off Mac's look for years. It was almost a joke that whatever outfit Mac debuted, Ruby Goldman would own one day later, or in the time it took to send her father's assistant on a shopping mission.

Mac sighed wistfully as she bent down to pick up a pair of Deener jeans. She'd been the first girl at BAMS to own a pair. She folded them and felt a sharp crease that didn't bend with the denim. And then she noticed: Poking out of a pocket was a piece of emerald green paper, folded into a very intricate origami bird.

TOP SECRET! To Ruby XOXO Haylie

Mac stared at the note, wondering what kind of secrets passed between the Rubybots. She was about to open it, but then realized she could never rearrange it back into the bird shape. Had Ruby even read it? She tucked it neatly into the back pocket and moved on to the sundresses just as she heard the bedroom door open.

"Mac, I'm back if you have any questions!" Ruby called from inside the room. "Just sending some e-mails 'cause I have to approve all these groups. I'll be so happy when this is over so I can run to Jamba Juice." She sighed. "I need another me."

"Okay, thanks!" Mac called, returning to her chore. It was almost fun to bring order to chaos, she realized.

Two hours later, she'd finished organizing Ruby's closet. The sections: jeans, pants, casual sweaters, dressy sweaters, day dresses, fancy dresses—were so clearly arranged by style and hue that a toddler could point to and pick a good outfit. Every item of clothing hung at least one inch apart from the other so the materials could "breathe." The task had been strangely, surprisingly Zen, which was why Mac hadn't realized so much time had passed. She sighed wistfully, looking at her handiwork. For a moment she wondered if she'd done *too* good a job. The last thing she wanted to discover was that her one true talent was being an assistant.

"Hey, Ruby!" Mac called. "Come take a look at your brand-new super-organized closet!"

Ruby hobbled over to the closet and leaned against the doorway. Her face looked pained and confused, as if she were seeing the Third World for the first time. Finally she sighed. "Oh, shoooot. I wanted it organized by *designer*."

Mac froze. "But you said—"

"I have to go interview a DJ!" Ruby cut her off, hobbling out on her crutches.

Mac pursed her lips and put her hands on her hips. The rules of the game were coming into crystal-clear focus, like downtown L.A. after a rainfall. No matter what she did, it wasn't going to be good enough.

Mac stood alone in the middle of Ruby's closet. For several seconds she was too frustrated to move. Then she bent down to pick up a Christian Louboutin sandal. She threw it angrily at the ground. Looking at the shimmering shoe on the closet floor, Mac wanted to step on it, but as she raised her foot she couldn't quite bring herself to injure a Louboutin, not even if it belonged to Ruby Goldman. And then she noticed Ruby's iPhone on the shelf by the door, blinking like a broken traffic light.

Mac gasped. How in the world could Ruby have been so stupid as to leave her iPhone *alone with her rival*? In plain sight? Mac imagined scrolling through Ruby's voice mails, or sending out e-mails. Her heart soared at the perfect prank potential. It would be so easy to pay Ruby back with the click of a few buttons. She picked up the phone, imagining typing an all-BAMS e-mail that would look like it came from Ruby: *Hey, everyone, I have a serious brain disorder and can't comprehend any spoken words over two syllables. Please address me in sign language or via written messages. If you must speak to me, please be respectful, as overly complicated wording causes an unfortunate reaction in which my drool ducts release and I go into attack mode.* Mac giggled, but then she remembered her mom's words: *It's all about respect*. Sometimes being classy was such a burden.

And sending a prank e-mail would be a very disrespectful thing to do.

Mac sighed and put the phone down sadly. She went back to her task, reaching for a Moschino sundress to place right next to a Marchesa silk wrap dress just as Ruby bounded back into her bedroom. "Back here if you need me!" Ruby hobbled over to the closet, where Mac was hard at work. "Hey, Mac," Ruby said, in that sweet voice. "DJ Aoki is good, right?"

Mac nodded.

"Great, that's what I thought. I just wanted to see if you thought so too." And Ruby hobbled out of the closet.

An hour later, when Ruby's wardrobe was newly, amazingly organized for the second time, Mac called out, "Hey, Ruby. It's arranged from *A* to *Z*!"

From her bedroom, Ruby yelled back. "Oh, boooo. I wanted it by *season*." She didn't even bother to look at Mac's work.

Mac balled her fists in frustration. Her lower back was starting to hurt, her fresh manicure was chipped, and she had been there for hours.

"Sure thing. By season," Mac hollered, even though that made no sense. There were really only two seasons in L.A.: *this* and *last*. But no way would Mac give Ruby the satisfaction of seeing her upset.

"MAAAAC," Ruby called. "Could you please, please come out here for a second?"

Mac groaned and headed out to the bedroom, where Ruby was hunched over her computer, looking at jpegs of flowers. "What do you think?" Ruby asked helplessly. "For the ExtravaBAMSa centerpiece?"

Mac surveyed the flowers. One was a tacky bouquet of roses and lilies. Another seemed obvio but was too simple: just daisies. The third choice, a simple assortment of white tulips, was just right. "That one." Mac pointed to the last image.

"Great, we agree," Ruby said fake-nicely. "Ooh, and could you tie my shoe?"

Mac winced in pain as she bent down for what felt like the hundredth time that day to tie the laces on Ruby's silver-trimmed Alice + Olivia sneakers.

"I'm having so much fun." Mac smiled, looking right into Ruby's narrow eyes.

"Great," Ruby said calmly, clicking on the Mac-selected image of flowers. "That makes me so happy." She looked up and faced Mac.

They stared at each other in a fake-smiling standoff. They both knew they were totally lying.

"Well, I'm going to meet with a photographer from

WireImage," Ruby said. She reached for her crutches and left the room, closing the door behind her.

Ping.

Mac looked over at the desk. Ruby had left her laptop wide open, her screen saver—of a bunny in a pink hat—totally exposed to the world. The pinging continued, and Mac realized Ruby was being instant-messaged. Mac closed her eyes, trying to remind herself of why she could not, could not, could not peek at the chat. . . . It was about paying her dues. And showing respect. Snooping did not show respect. She angled her body in the guise of "stretching" toward the door. And then, just as she was about to give in to temptation and click on Ruby's keyboard to read the instant message, Ruby smacked in the door with her right crutch. Mac jerked her hand away from the computer keyboard. Thankfully, the screen was still on sleep mode.

"Forgot to tell you something," Ruby said. "You should log my wardrobe and then take the log home with you to reassess." She looked down at the pinging computer and then back at Mac, seemingly unbothered. "I don't want you wearing anything that I own. Overlapping is just so LY, you know?"

Mac couldn't even stop herself. "Ruby, that's just stupid," she snapped. "You copy everything I own. We have the same wardrobe."

Ruby leaned in, but then remembered her ankle wasn't strong enough to support her. "You know what's stupid?" She steadied herself on her crutch. "Getting *thisclose* and screwing your friends *again*."

Mac stared at Ruby, thankful there were no witnesses to this transaction. "So just make a list of everything. . . ." Ruby continued talking, but Mac wasn't listening. She was calculating what she owned that Ruby hadn't already ripped off: the Vanessa Bruno jumpsuit (not yet debuted?) or the Donatella Versace sweater dress (Donatella had only given away twenty-five to friends and family) or the Loomstate organic dresses (Ruby wasn't making eco-friendly choices).

"By the way, what's a great place for a party?" Ruby asked sweetly.

Mac blinked. Ruby switched gears faster than a Ferrari.

"The Getty Museum," Mac said, without thinking.

"Great, see you at the Getty this Saturday," Ruby said. "You're the party butler. And here's your uniform." She smiled, handing Mac a black and white maid's uniform just like the one Mac had seen on Ruby's maid.

Mac mentally rewound, realizing she'd just heard the words *you, party,* and *butler* in a sentence that was not a joke. She blinked several times, too shocked to speak.

"Whaaaa?" Mac finally asked, making a face like she'd tasted airline coffee.

"I need you at the Getty around seven to serve."

A vision flashed in Mac's mind: spending Saturday night waiting on the Rubybots? What would they do?

Spray themselves with fake tan? Discuss more ways to copy the Inner Circle? Mac shivered. Besides the fact that she didn't want to have to spend time with those people, there was a bigger problem: Mac's private humiliation was about to go public.

CHAPTER SIXTEEN

emily

◀ Friday September 11 ▶

7:30 AM	Hello, Spazmo. Ugh. Get ready for school (glasses? Check. World's ugliest flannel? Check. Huge sense of embarrassment? Check)
8 AM	Spanish class
12 PM	Lunch (where can I be invisible?)
3 PM	Get to be EMILY again
6:30 PM	iChat Paige (I still hate iChat)

Emily tiptoed nervously into her first day of Señorita Lumley's Spanish class, walking as quickly as she could so people wouldn't have time to actually see her. Which was an impossible goal when you were dressed as Spazmo. She was totally *loca,* wearing crazy glasses, the ugly red plaid flannel that looked like it hadn't been washed since the '70s, and (used—ugh!) headgear. What was worse, Spanish class was only once a week, which meant that the whole *class* would be seeing her for the first time, as Spazmo.

Spanish class was in the modern wing, a row of classrooms off Main Quad used for foreign language classes. All the desks were equipped with headsets so students could practice speaking with audio CD-ROMs, and they were arranged in a giant U so that everyone faced each other. When Emily entered, the classroom became so silent that Emily could hear the second hand on the clock actually ticking.

She could feel everyone in the class trying not to stare at the odd girl. She noticed kids shooting her curious, uncomfortable glances and then quickly averting their eyes. Even Señorita Lumley forced herself to look away, focusing her gaze on the *Bienvenidos a Barcelona* poster of the famous Gaudi church on the back wall. Emily slid into a seat near the back door, opening her Spanish workbook wide to hide her face.

Just before the clock struck eight, Kimmie Tachman slunk into the last seat right next to Emily. She turned her head to the left so her frizzy ponytail hit her desk and whispered, "Love the outfit!" Emily smiled weakly and turned her attention to the center of the room.

Señorita Lumley shook her green maracas to get the class's attention. "*Buenos*! *Dias*! *Clase*! Welcome to your first day of Spanish class!" Her Spanish had a very thick American accent, even if she had perfect grammar. She had poofy red hair, which she coated in a helmet of hair spray, and freckles, and she looked like she was probably thirty-five. "There is a name tag on your desk. Please write your name and wear this name tag so I can get to know all of you."

Emily picked up her pen and was about to write *Emily*, but then she spotted Kimmie grinning at her mischievously, and she wrote *Spazmo* instead.

"Today we are going to introduce ourselves *en español*," Señorita Lumley said excitedly. She sounded proud of her assignment.

Emily groaned, a little too loud.

Señorita Lumley whipped her focus to Emily. "*Hay una problema*?"

Emily blushed. She hadn't meant to complain—she just didn't want a group of people to meet her as Spazmo.

"You can go first and get it over with." Señorita Lumley smiled.

Emily shot the teacher a *please don't do this to me* look, but it was either lost behind her ginormous freak glasses or Señorita Lumley didn't care.

"Sometime this school year!" Señorita Lumley waved the maracas at Emily.

Reluctantly, Emily stood up very slowly, too aware of the ticking sound from the clock in the super-quiet classroom. She spotted Lukas Gregory watching her with a curious smile, like someone was about to tell him a good joke. She wondered if he recognized her as Mac's friend. A girl next to him picked up her cell phone and surreptitiously began texting under her desk (cell phones weren't allowed in class). Emily wondered how many other people were gossiping about her, or were planning to.

Finally she spoke, making sure to use her androgynous voice and Spazmo-lisp. "*Hola. Me llamo Eh-mee-lee-a*." She stared down at her desk, kicking her Vans against each other. "*Venga de Iowa*."

Señorita Lumley put down her maracas and looked

at Emily sadly. The class was silent, and no one was laughing. Lukas Gregory had stopped smiling, and he looked bummed out. Surely the class knew this was a joke, right? Then Emily realized her worst fears had come true. These kids had never met her as Emily. They thought she really was Spazmo.

Kimmie cleared her throat from the desk next to Emily. She scribbled something on her pink notebook and turned her notebook so Emily could read. It said, *METHOD!*

Emily took a deep breath and began again. "*Soy El Spazmo,*" she said, this time with even more of a lisp, so it came out *Thpathmo*. "*Me encanta Los Angeles.*"

Next to Emily, a tiny brunette whose name tag said MINKA smiled encouragingly at Emily. Thank goodness someone gets the joke, Emily thought. She winked at Minka, just to show that she was in on it. Minka looked a little startled but smiled back.

Suddenly the sea of horrified faces staring at Emily was too unbearable. She needed to escape this torture chamber. Emily raised her hand. "*Puedo ir al baño?*"

Señorita Lumley nodded somberly.

Emily walked quickly to the bathroom, not looking up. She raced into a stall and leaned her back against the door, staring up at the baby blue ceiling. She felt totally friendless and freakish.

Thankfully, she had her iPhone with her. She pulled it out of her Diesel jeans pocket and called the one person she knew would be happy to hear her voice. The phone rang once.

"Baby, what's wrong?" Lori Mungler spoke soothingly into the phone.

"Hi, Mom! Nothing's wrong," Emily said, so relieved to hear her mom's voice.

"Oh, please! I don't believe you're calling dear old Mom in the middle of the school day because everything's just peachy." Emily imagined her mother standing over their honey-colored kitchen counter. She was probably on her fourth cup of black tea, watching *Dr. Phil* until her shift at the hospital began. Her mother was an emergency room nurse and she worked nights. "Are classes hard?"

"No. Classes are fine. It's just that . . . " Emily took a deep breath, ready to spill about Kimmie and Pax Rubana. Then her mom would tell her everything was going to be all right, and it would be.

Just when Emily was about to unleash her emotions, the bathroom door clicked and she heard that all-too-familiar singsongy voice.

"Method!" Kimmie Tachman called from the sinks.

"Is everything going okay out there?" Lori asked. "Because if it's not . . ."

Emily closed her eyes, not listening to her mother. She felt like a fugitive who had just been caught. She could run but she could not hide from the Tawker.

"Thorry, I have to go," Emily whispered into her

phone. She could never explain this all to her mother with Kimmie eavesdropping.

"What? I can't hear you!" Lori said.

"Thorry!"

"Why are you speaking with a speech impediment?" Lori asked.

"Creth Whitethrips!" Emily whispered, holding her phone close to her mouth.

"But why are you wearing them at school?" Lori sounded completely confused.

"I love you! Gotta go!" Emily said, and put her iPhone back into her pocket. She sat on the closed toilet seat in her jeans, not ready to face Kimmie Tachman.

As far as she could tell, she only had two options:

1. Stay in Bel-Air and be a total loser who should have stayed in Iowa.
2. Return to Iowa as the total loser who failed in Bel-Air.

Her choices were lame and lamer, and she wasn't sure which was which. All she knew was that, like the green gum on the back of the bathroom stall, she was *muy, muy* stucko.

Finally she heard the door close and she was sure that Kimmie was gone. Emily crept out of the stall and stared at herself in the bathroom mirror. It was like looking at a stranger. Even she didn't recognize herself behind the black frames, the huge shirt that made her look like a refrigerator box, and the headgear. She sighed, remembering Mac's pep talk and Pax Rubana. If Coco, Mac, and Becks could lower themselves to work as assistants, then surely Emily could do *this* to pay her dues. She dabbed some water on her face and headed out.

The first person Emily spotted when she stepped into the hallway was Mac, thwopping down the hallway in her Havaiana flip-flops, her blond hair flowing down the back of her Nanette Lepore sundress. Emily smiled. They were both on a bathroom break at the same time! The first stroke of good luck all day.

Emily eagerly walked toward Mac, who stared ahead, ignoring her.

"Hi, Mac! Emily cried.

Mac smiled uncomfortably. It was the kind of fake, nanosecond smile that Mac flashed to non–Inner Circle people.

And then Emily realized: Mac didn't even recognize her!

Emily grabbed Mac's arm. "Hey, it's me! Emily!"

Mac stared for a long time, like Emily was a puzzle she was trying to mentally assemble. "Wow," she said finally. "You're really transformed."

"Oh no," Emily sighed. "Is it really that bad?"

"You're doing great! Stick with it," Mac said, in full Adrienne mode. Just then, her gaze landed on something in the distance. She arched her shoulders. "I should go," she said, turning toward the bathroom. "I'm missing class."

Emily turned to see what had caught Mac's attention: Lukas Gregory was walking toward them. And *she* was making Mac look like a loser by association. Emily looked like such a freak that her best friend in Bel-Air was embarrassed to be seen with her.

Emily hung her head and crawled back into Spanish class, wishing it—like her Bel-Air experience—would be over *pronto*.

CHAPTER seventeen

COCO

◀ Friday September 11 ▶

11:45 AM Dance practice. Bleh

Coco walked into the BAMS dance studio wearing a Michael Stars V-neck Henley over Ksubi super-skinny jeans. She inhaled the lavender room freshener and sweat smell just as the Bam-Bams were beginning their stretches. They stood in a row, one leg on the barre, arms over their heads, wearing matching navy blue hoodies and Lululemon pants with a pink band around the hips. Spotting Coco, Haylie picked up a pile of clothes from the floor and walked over.

"I want you to feel like you're part of the team," Haylie said, hoisting the bundle at Coco. Haylie's hoodie said CAPTAIN in lowercase letters. "I had this made for you."

Coco opened the ball of clothing excitedly. All her hard work had paid off, and she knew that once she put on her matching hoodie, she'd finally feel like she was back on the team. But when she unraveled the bundle, her heart plummeted as she realized it didn't match the other members' outfits—it was a navy blue tracksuit jacket and giant pants. When she held up the jacket, the back read WATER BOY. Yes, WATER *BOY*, in giant Arial font lettering. There could be no mistaking Coco's lame new title.

But it was only for one more week, Coco reminded herself as she put the enormous tracksuit on over her clothes. She headed to her water station in the corner of the studio. She reached under the table to retrieve a Voss bottle, her knees cracking as she bent down. A giant tub of industrial soap and a huge sponge had been placed on the floor, with a Post-it that said, *Coco, please scrub floor*. Coco rolled her eyes.

"All righty, girls! Water break!" Haylie bellowed to the room. "And we're back in five!"

As the Bam-Bams trickled by to grab their waters, Coco felt totally invisible. When Eden Singer reached for her special-requested Voss, she didn't even look at Coco, let alone say thank you.

"Good job out there, Eden," Coco chirped. She meant it, but she sounded like a total suck-up. She was so desperate to have someone to talk to. "You looked like you were having fun."

"Uh . . . thanks?" Eden said tentatively, looking around as if she didn't want to be seen talking to Coco.

Coco jerked back in surprise. Since when did Eden blow her off? Coco was so scarred by that, she didn't even bother trying to make small talk with the other girls, who certainly didn't initiate conversation with her. Why did they have to hate her? Wasn't she paying her dues by working this lame job? Or did that only make them think she was a kiss-up? She wondered if Haylie had instructed them not to talk to her . . . or if she was so far beneath them that they were choosing not to themselves.

Coco put her head down and went back to arranging the waters on the foldout table while the Bam-Bams rehearsed for ExtravaBAMSa, drilling their pirated version of Coco's captain audition. Half curiously, half pityingly, she watched the train wreck that the Bam-Bams had become: Since they were all doing exactly the same dance (hers!), there was no one movement that took focus, and they kept almost colliding. They looked like the Slam-Slams. Coco cringed. It *almost* made her glad she wasn't part of the team.

Coco double-checked herself to make sure she wasn't being a bitter captain-turned-water-boy, but it was pretty clear that Haylie wasn't helping things. She'd placed herself in the center of the group: a huge, pale eyesore who really didn't move well. She was always a beat off from the other girls, which in turn made everyone else doubt their counts.

"Good job, girls, you're really getting this!" Haylie said. She stood in front of the group, pulling her wife-beater down over her belly so no skin was exposed. She turned her baby blue Von Dutch trucker hat sideways.

Coco looked around the room. Judging by the disillusioned looks on their faces, the Bam-Bams knew they weren't getting it. Eden Singer was staring down at the wood panels on the dance floor. Maribel and Lucia's icy blue eyes looked like they were fighting back tears. Ames and Taylor seemed nervous, their faces scrunched up in confusion. Even though Haylie was trying to be inspirational, no one could take her dance opinions seriously. It was like taking fashion advice from Bai Ling.

"Girls, we're gonna rock!" Haylie grunted to the group. She seemed slightly unhinged by the steely eyes staring back at her. Her voice was defensive. "Look, girls, Ruby is in charge of approving the ExtravaBAMSa lineup, and this is the dance she wants," Haylie said threateningly. "It's this or nothing."

Coco checked the group for some reaction, but the girls were frozen in place on the dance floor. No one wanted Haylie as dance captain, but no one was brave enough to say anything. Coco sighed. She could never understand herd mentality.

"Coco, don't forget to leave my water near the stereo this time!" Haylie said gruffly. "I don't have time to keep running over to your corner."

Coco clenched her teeth into a fake smile that didn't fool anyone. But she didn't snap anything nasty back at Haylie. She didn't want to blow it for the I.C. when they'd already invested so much time in Pax Rubana.

"And another thing, Coco," Haylie said. She didn't

even try to sound nice. "Get a notepad—you might want to write this down."

Coco obediently reached into her oversize zebra-stripe bag and pulled out a green gel roller and a pink Hello Kitty notebook, making a silent vow that if she were *ever* in a position to boss anyone around, she would always say *please* and *thank you* and speak in a sweet voice.

Haylie put her hands on her hips. Coco couldn't stop staring at how white Haylie's hands were or how exposed Haylie's muffin-top was. "We're going to need you to tape practices, and then you can upload them and e-mail them at a good file size. Lucia and Maribel need Vitamin Water citrus flavor, *not* whatever you've been getting. Taylor has requested Pellegrino, *not* Fiji. Eden wants a Diet Coke in addition to her Fiji, which she would like chilled—but not with ice—and we're gonna need at least four Red Bulls and three kombuchas. Also, we'd like some dried Bing cherries, two Strawberries Wild Jamba Juice smoothies with a shot of wheatgrass in one and an immunity boost in the other, and a medium plain Pinkberry for everyone on the team. I'd like some potato chips, and I don't care what kind you get as long as they have antioxidants." Haylie smiled. "Oh, and we'd like everything served on an eco-friendly bamboo tray within the hour."

Coco fake-smiled. "No prob," she lied. The only thing that gave Coco the strength to fake-smile was the knowledge that the Inner Circle was suffering with her. She knew that Mac had been Ruby's whipping girl, that Becks had been struggling with Ellie, and that Emily had to be Spazmo. If they all had to play those parts, then Coco could handle some obnoxious speed-shopping.

"See you in an hour!" Coco smiled and headed out of the room. The second she stepped outside the dance studio, she called her mother's butler, Pablo, who zoomed up the hill. He promptly drove her down to Beverly Hills, where she ran like a lunatic through town crossing off half her list while Pablo took the other half.

Fifty-eight minutes later, Pablo dropped Coco off in front of the BAMS gates, and she returned breathlessly to the dance studio, her right shoulder aching from lugging so many snacks and drinks. She was pleased that she'd managed to fill a next-to-impossible request in the allotted time. And she'd already taught herself how to tape and download dance routines, because she'd done that with Marcel this summer in London.

"That's it for today; we'll regroup tomorrow!" Haylie barked, tucking her Von Dutch trucker hat low across her eyes. Then, spotting Coco, she muttered to the group, "Snacks are here if you want them."

So much for the need to have it done in an hour, Coco thought dryly. But after hearing about how Mac had had to redo Ruby's closet three times, she knew the Rubybots were all about making power plays.

The Bam-Bams spilled out to the corners of the room

to gather their things, while Haylie stood in the center of the room running through the choreography on her own. She took a step, then started a double pirouette. She stopped mid-spin in a jerky landing when she realized Coco was staring at her.

"Um, Haylie, can I talk to you for a second?" Coco asked.

"Yeeesss, Coco?" Haylie pulled her hat down lower and looked at her.

Coco played with the zipper on her tracksuit jacket and shifted nervously from her left foot to her right. "I was just wondering . . . I know I'm not supposed to rejoin the team before ExtravaBAMSa, but I have a suggestion about the performance."

"What do you mean, *rejoin the team*?" Haylie asked, confused. The second Coco saw the blank look in Haylie's cold blue eyes she instantly regretted her decision to confront the girl. She wished she'd called or e-mailed or somehow never given Haylie the gift of being able to put her down in person. But she'd gone so far down that road she had no choice but to stand there and wait.

"Just, you know, when I get to rejoin the team?" Coco prompted.

"Hmm . . . I don't know what you're talking about?" Haylie said. Her confusion looked real.

"The deal . . . you know . . . I do this until ExtravaBAMSa and then I get to . . ." Coco stopped talking because Haylie was still shaking her head, confused.

Coco looked away, fixing her eyes on the glowing red EXIT sign above the door.

Finally Haylie spoke. "I feel like there's been a *misunderstanding*."

"Oh, I get it!" Coco said quickly, just to end the conversation. But as she shoved her hands into the pockets of her tracksuit and made her way to the door, she understood one thing all too clearly: She was nowhere near done. And she had a feeling that Pax Rubana wasn't as up front and simple as Mac had made it out to be.

CHAPTER EIGHTEEN

mac

◀ Saturday September 12 ▶

2 PM	Acupuncture to de-stress
6:30 PM	Arrive @ the Getty Museum
9 PM	Leave and go to Inner Circle sleepover (seriously, how long can this take?)

"What do *you* think, Mac?" Erin turned and stared at Mac, her green eyes bugging behind her diamond-studded cat-eye glasses. Mac realized Erin was *still* talking about the films of Barry Goldman. Somehow Erin had confused Mac's Need for a Car Ride with An Invitation to Reenact *Ebert & Roeper.*

"I'm sorry, I wasn't listening." Mac reached into the glove compartment to grab a Red Bull. She flashed Erin an *I'm just being polite* smile, but Erin wasn't people-savvy enough to pick up on it. She had no social radar. Erin pushed up the sleeves on her purple Talbots turtleneck, which, for some strange reason, she'd paired with a red Patagonia fleece.

"Barry Goldman's movies," Erin continued emphatically. "They're just *soooo* formulaic." She lowered the volume on her soft-rock flute CD, which was flowing through the car. "He casts hot eighteen-year-old girls to play rocket scientists and then makes them run around in tight tank tops so their boobs bounce." Erin rolled her eyes. "Not that you can't be smart and hot, but come on." She unzipped her fleece. "I mean, by the time you'd finish your Ph.D., gotten practical training, and built up enough of a reputation to be leading a CIA mission, you'd be *at least* thirty-six." Mac shot Erin another *just being polite* smile, but Erin missed it again. At least she was consistent. "What do you think, Mac?"

"I guess so," Mac said. The conversation would end faster if she just agreed. Mac stared out the window at the eucalyptus trees as they turned off the 405 Freeway and onto the road leading up to the Getty Museum, which was located on a high hill in Brentwood overlooking Los Angeles.

Normally Mac enjoyed the Getty. She sometimes did homework in the café because the view of the gardens de-stressed her before tests. But tonight, all she wanted was to finish her night's duties as Ruby's PB (Party Butler). Then Erin could drive her to Becks's house for the Inner Circle's Saturday night sleepover and her fun could finally begin.

As the Prius cruised higher up the hill and the stark white concrete museum came closer into view, Mac began predicting the guest list. It was a challenge, because Ruby had never actually had friends before this year. Mac guessed: Kimmie, Ellie, Haylie. And a wild card. (Eden Singer? She was a social climber.) Mac sighed. All those girls had one thing in common: They were just *beneath* her. And yet here she was, listening to Erin's flute soft rock, and a never-ending rant on the misogyny in Barry Goldman's films, dressed in a polyester maid's uniform and getting ready to be their party butler.

It was almost a comedy, except that it was her life. The *only* good thing about the maid's uniform was that she hadn't had to search for an outfit Ruby didn't own, yet another deal point that had been hanging over her all that week like a storm cloud.

Mac walked to the front door of the restaurant, which Ruby had rented out—weird, since it was a pretty big space. Ruby greeted her at the door, balanced on her crutches, wearing a turquoise half-sleeve Juicy Couture dress that had *just* gone on Shopbop.com that very morning.

"Follow me," Ruby ordered. Then she turned and swung into the party area.

Mac's jaw dropped open as she realized the party wasn't just the Rubybots + a Random. Ruby's party was *packed*.

Mac started to feel a little dizzy, and it wasn't just the glare bouncing off the wall-to-ceiling windows, the strobe light Ruby had focused on the makeshift dance floor (ew), or the fast beat of the pop music blaring through hidden speakers. The sea of faces went blurry as her eyes darted around the L-shaped room, which overlooked the Getty gardens.

Some of the Bam-Bams—Eden Singer and the Peet twins—wore matching Petro Zillia silk mini jumpers, and sipped orange-colored drinks. Petra Rockets (child model) and Matilda Summers (guitar player) were lounging on a giant white sofa. On the far right side of the room, Khloe Divonne (Green Club president) and Nika Alexander (girl who always referred to herself as an heiress) were playing Dance Dance Revolution on a giant screen. She realized that Ruby had invited THEIR ENTIRE GRADE.

Mac's heart beat even faster when she spotted the soccer boys throwing pita chips at each other. Jaden and Slate Shean (even *they* were invited?!?!) were standing on the deck, awkwardly pretending to play hopscotch but really just drawing on the ground with chalk. Mac's gaze flitted around the room, searching frantically for the one boy she hoped most of all wouldn't be there. But sure enough, in the back, staring at her with an amused twinkle in his dark eyes, was Lukas Gregory. Even worse, he was flanked by his water polo teammates Hunter Crowe and Moses Ridgely. So his whole group of friends could witness what a tool she was. Mac's heartbeat screeched to a halt. How could this be happening to *her*?

Mac looked down and remembered she was wearing her maid's uniform. Of all the times she'd perfected her ensembles just so Lukas could see her—of course she had to run into him on a day when she looked like *staff*. Mac plastered a fake smile on her face just so she didn't cry.

She stood still and felt the eyes of her entire grade on her. And every face said the same thing: *What is Mac Armstrong doing here, dressed like that?*

Ruby pulled out a cordless microphone. "Hey, peoples, do you all know Mackenzie Little-Armstrong?" she asked sweetly, as though everyone had social amnesia and had forgotten the past five years, during which Mac had been the most popular girl in school.

Mac made an insta-decision to smile and *embrace the moment*, knowing that to back off on eye contact now would only make her look pathetic, and—worse—like Ruby was the one running the show. Mac had to look strong—she was representing the Inner Circle. She twirled the I.C. ring at the end of her necklace for strength.

"Hey, everyone," Mac said sweetly. She cheerfully put a hand on her maid's uniform, like it was the latest fashion craze and she was posing for the paparazzi. If she was going to get a ton of attention for something embarrassing, she was going to look as cute as possible doing it.

"Mac is helping me out tonight," Ruby cooed to the group as though they were a bunch of preschoolers. "So if you need anything—refills, extra snacks—just let her know!"

Everyone looked confused, as if Ruby had just spoken

in Japanese. "Why?" asked Maya Hulse (soccer player), her head tilted in confusion.

Mac cringed, hoping Ruby wouldn't drop the A-bomb. Still, she kept her smile, like a politician at election time.

"Because she's my assistant!" Ruby said proudly, beaming at Mac as though it were a dream come true for them both. Mac felt like a new purse dog being shown off to the group. And that feeling was her intuition telling her to bolt. "I gotta get to work," Mac said, glancing toward the kitchen. It was time to leave this freak show, of which she was the star.

Mac waited alone in the Getty café's industrial kitchen, which had white-tiled walls and silver appliances. Since Ruby had rented out the space, the Getty staff had gone home for the evening. In the middle of the kitchen was a shiny silver counter with three large trays of food, which Mac assumed she would be serving. She leaned against the counter and sent desperate text messages to the I.C.: RED ALERT! ENTIRE GRADE IS HERE! AACK!

Emily's text came first: AT LEAST ENTIRE GRADE KNOWS U R SRY?

Mac laughed at her friend's sweet yet naïve effort to see the bright side.

Coco got it: THAT BLOWZ. And so did Becks: WORD.

Mac was about to respond when Ruby appeared. "All right, I know you don't want to be here," Ruby said matter-of-factly. Mac noticed Ruby was wearing wooden bangles—*Mac's* signature item. She made a mental note to switch to silver bangles. "So all you have to do is serve the food, course by course, and then go."

Mac mentally calculated the task ahead. Three courses x 15 minutes per course = 45 minutes. She'd be at Becks's house well before nine! At least Ruby had some heart.

"The thing is, we need to try everything because we're testing the menu for ExtravaBAMSa," Ruby said, pointing to the three trays of food. "I know we discussed this earlier, but I still can't even decide if I want to go with Joan's on Third or The Little Next Door." Ruby shrugged. "Seriah-sly, be glad you're not social chair."

Mac almost rolled her eyes but didn't take the bait. She knew Ruby was trying very, very hard to push her buttons. She leaned against the silver countertop and played with the Inner Circle ring at the end of her silver chain.

"I want every guest to feel important, so what that means is that you have to offer every single person every single item. No drop-the-tray-and-run kind of thing," Ruby warned. "Or we can just call the whole thing off."

Mac nodded. All she wanted was to do the work and get out of there and be with her friends.

Ruby pointed to a silver tray with rippled edges. "Mini cupcakes," she said. "We also have mini chocolate fondants." She pointed to a shiny gold hatbox in the corner, which Mac hadn't noticed. "Flown in from Maison du Chocolat, *merci beaucoup*." Ruby smirked.

Mac wasn't thinking about airborne chocolates. She looked at her silver Baume & Mercier watch. It was seven fifteen. She clenched her fists determinedly. If she hustled, she might actually make the Inner Circle's movie, which this week was an advance super-top-secret release of the uncut version of Davey Woodward's blockbuster summer movie, *Time Bomb*.

"All right," Mac said, clenching her teeth and removing the saran wrap from the mini cupcakes.

"Oh, and one more thing . . ." Ruby placed her iPhone on the counter and walked to the industrial-size fridge. Mac had been so busy texting her friends that she hadn't thought to peek inside. Ruby opened the fridge and waved inside like a *Deal or No Deal* beauty opening her suitcase. "You should probably start with all this."

Mac gulped. She tiptoed over to the refrigerator and peered inside. It had at least ten huge shelves of *even more food*. There were tiny folded signs above each tray, spelling out in calligraphy what each dish was. Shiitake mushroom polenta cakes. Manchego bruschetta. Portobello mushroom quesadillas. Low-fat spanakopita with feta and ricotta. Pancetta-and-leek tartlet. Chinese scallion pancackes. Thai chicken satay. Sea bass skewers. Baked Brie with pecans and green apples. And on and on and on. Mac's workload had just gone from one hour to five.

Mac death-gripped her phone in her pocket, seconds away from texting Erin and begging her to pick her up and end this misery. But then she remembered Ruby's promise, and how this would restore her friends' place in the BAMS hierarchy. She had to pay these crappy dues for them, despite the pain.

"Is that all?" Mac said, faking nonchalance.

Ruby bit her lower lip and smiled like she was looking at a toddler's scribbles. "Well played, Mac." She smiled. "Yes, that's all." She hobbled out the door on her crutches, leaving Mac to stare at the endless array of catered food.

Mac sighed but promptly got to work. She decided to start with the quesadillas, which were stuffed with portobello mushrooms, goat cheese, and dates, and were sprinkled with a touch of Asiago cheese. She inhaled the buttery aroma, wishing she were eating, not serving.

Mac hoisted the enormous silver platter onto her shoulder and headed to the expansive, glass-walled party room, plastering another huge fake smile on her face. Now the BAMS kids were dancing to an electronic version of Miley Cyrus's "Girls Night Out." Ruby was standing in the center of the room, in the middle of a circle of Rubybots, with a bored smile on her face, barely moving her hips from side to side while she danced. Kimmie Tachman, Ellie Parker, and Haylie moved around her. They looked like they were trying to look bored. But they probably didn't have to try very hard.

Mac walked carefully around the partygoers like she was stepping around land mines. Her BAMS classmates were talking in huddled groups or sprawled out on lush red chaises and couches that lined the edges of the L-shaped room. She gingerly placed a tray of quesadillas in front of each person like she'd seen waiters do at her parents' parties. "Goat cheese quesadilla?" She cringed when she got to Lukas and the water polo boys, who were on a couch by the floor-to-ceiling windows.

"You havin' a good time?" he asked, his brown eyes twinkling. His hair was mussed in that perfect stylish/ effortless way that some guys could pull off naturally.

"Sure," Mac said. What could she say? That she felt like a total loser? That she probably *was* a total loser? "This rocks."

"I'll bet," Lukas said, laughing.

Mac wasn't sure if he was laughing with her or at her as she blushed and hurried back to the kitchen, the empty tray feeling even heavier now than when it was loaded.

At first, the BAMS kids seemed baffled by (and almost scared of?) Mac's goodwill, like they were on *Pop Fiction*. For Mac, it was torture to stand there while her social inferiors practically ignored her. Each tray seemed to take forever to finish.

Once, when she was holding a tray of tartlets on her shoulder, she had to wait for an extra ten minutes while

Jaden and Slate debated whether or not they wanted another. Mac did her best to hide her scowl, knowing full well they were just trying to be obnoxious. But she had made a mental note to pass by them with the other sixteen trays.

Somehow, five hours, thirty-five trays, and plenty of A-level humiliation later, Mac was done. She stood alone in the Getty kitchen, her arms feeling weak and gelatinous. She hugged herself to stretch out her aching biceps. She wished she could magically transport herself to Becks's house for the Inner Circle slumber party. She leaned against the silver refrigerator and closed her eyes, tuning out the squeals of laughter from the party. And then she noticed: Ruby's cell phone was by the tray of mini cupcakes.

And it was blinking.

It would be so easy to peek into the phone/read her messages/respond to texts or seriously sabotage Ruby. She imagined sending the Rubybots text messages from Ruby's phone. Like: U GUYS! I HEART THE SHEAN TWINS! Or better yet: EVERYONE B NICE TO MAC. She could order them to stop dressing the same. Mac smiled wistfully at the fantasy, and then realized she was wasting time instead of changing out of her maid getup. She wandered into a bathroom to put on her Habitual jeans.

When she turned on the lights, she realized she hadn't walked into the bathroom—she'd walked into a giant pantry, stocked with rows and rows of Barilla pasta and tall, thin bottles of extra-virgin olive oil with curved silver spouts. Mac was about to leave and find the real bathroom when she heard hushed voices just outside the door.

"I can't believe she's working for you!" a girl said. Mac froze. She tilted her body so she could peer out the door. It was Ruby and Maya Hulse, a BAMS soccer star, sticking their fingers in the leftover mini cupcakes and eating the chocolate icing. Ruby certainly seemed to have forgotten her diet.

"What happened to Mac? She used to rule BAMS, and now she's a party butler?" Maya continued. She was so tiny that even next to Ruby she still looked petite. Her brown hair was cut in a shag like Katie Holmes's and her brown bangs framed her wide-set eyes. She looked a little bit like a doll. "Mac really peaked last year. How sad."

"Times change." Ruby licked her index finger like a cat.

Mac squeezed a box of Barilla pasta to keep from bursting out of the closet and throttling Ruby. But that would end the conversation, and she had to remind herself of the basic rule of Hollywood: Information was power. (Side bonus: If Ruby kept eating icing like that, she would sabotage herself).

"And you should see what I'm doing to her little project, Emily," Ruby chuckled. "Let's just say . . . stay tuned for Spazmo."

"That was you?" Maya asked, incredulously. "I heard Kimmie's really into that play." She tossed a cupcake back onto the tray and reached for a quesadilla.

"Duh. She is. Kimmie can't be mean." Ruby snickered. "But all she has to do is make people watch her play. That's torture enough."

So this was how Ruby talked about her "friends."

"Shhh!" Maya giggled. "Kimmie will hear you!"

"I hope she does." Ruby rolled her eyes. "Someone needs to save her from herself. She actually thinks she's going to be a writer. Can you say delusional?"

"You're totally running BAMS!" Maya squeaked. "Is that why Haylie is dance captain?"

"Let's just say every skinny girl needs a big BFF." Ruby tossed the rest of the cupcake back into the tray. "Standing next to her is the fastest way I know to look ten pounds skinnier."

"You are cra-zee!" Maya teased. "So what's next for Team Mac?"

Ruby lowered her voice. "Believe me when I say this is only the beginning."

The beginning? Mac froze, still clutching the now-mangled box of pasta. Wasn't this all supposed to be over at ExtravaBAMSa?

The girls turned and went back to the party, leaving Mac simmering alone in the pantry. As quietly as she could, Mac slid out of the closet, out of the kitchen, and finally out of the Getty.

Pax Rubana was a total sham. Ruby had never intended to honor her promises.

Erin was waiting in the Prius, eating dried mangoes with chili powder from a Whole Foods bag, when Mac slumped into the passenger seat.

"Hi, sweetie!" Erin said cheerfully.

Mac looked at her mom's personal assistant with new eyes. Suddenly she didn't see Erin as a girl who over-quoted Oprah—she saw her as a Brave Survivor. Erin ran errands, took coffee orders, and schlepped the Armstrong family every single day, never complaining. "*How* can you stand your job, Erin? It's like being a servant!"

"Yeeaahhh," Erin sighed melodically. It went on for many syllables, like she was warming up for a concert. "It can be rough." She smile-nodded.

Mac stared at Erin. "No, seriously. How do you do it?"

Erin played with the pine tree–shaped air freshener hanging from the rearview mirror, probably debating how truthful she could be with her boss's daughter. "Okay. Honestly, there are days when I think, *I graduated from Princeton! Hello? What am I doing with my life?*"

Mac nodded. This made sense.

"But see, I wouldn't last if I thought of myself as a servant," Erin continued.

Mac scrunched her eyebrows in concentration, very curious as to how Erin spun her job.

"'Cause I'm *not* a servant," Erin added. "I'm a home

staffer with some cool perks." It made Mac a little sad to hear Erin's self-talk. "Don't tell your mom, but last night I got a reservation at Osteria Mozza just by saying I worked for Adrienne Little-Armstrong. I call it dropping the A-bomb. Works every time." Erin winked. "Aaaaaand I have access to really cool people. I know about big deals that go down. And how else would I be friends with you?"

Mac smiled. Even if it was just Erin, at least someone still thought she was cool.

Erin started the car. "Plus, when you're an assistant, people forget you exist. They say things in front of you they would never say around anyone else. I mean, if I were *a different* kind of person"—Erin looked at Mac intently, narrowing her eyes mock-sinisterly—"I could do some real damage."

"Like what?" Mac asked, suddenly interested in the *damage* of it all: She thought back to all the conversations she'd heard that night. And all the conversations she could have heard at Ruby's house if she'd made that her goal.

"I mean—I would neh-ver do this—but you know, I *could* call up the tabloids or write a tell-all book under a fake name. I could even turn my experiences into a one-woman show. I could just really abuse all this access. Thank goodness I'm not crazy." She winked at Mac for the second time that conversation.

"Yeah," Mac said, not fully sold on the whole Erin-not-being-crazy thing, but she wasn't thinking about Erin. She was thinking about her future, and how she could go back to being the master of it, taking the reins from Ruby Goldman. Suddenly life became obvious, like the ending of a Katherine Heigl movie. There was no sense in playing by the rules if she and Ruby weren't even playing the same game. Screw sucking up. Mac smiled as the car sailed down Mulholland Drive, overlooking the twinkling sea of lights.

It was time to play hardball. Fortunately, that was Mac's favorite game.

CHAPTER nineteen

becks

◀ Saturday September 12 ▶

8 PM I.C. slumber party (at least something is still normal around here)

Becks passed a bag of Crummy Brothers orange blossom chocolate chip cookies to Emily and Coco, who each robotically reached into the brown paper bag and took one. They were sitting at the farmhouse picnic table in Becks's kitchen, which had been redesigned so that "chi could flow" (as Clutch put it). As far as Becks could tell, there were just more bamboo shoots dotting the emerald green granite island.

They sipped their ginger wheatgrass smoothies, which had been graciously forced upon them by Clutch, who joyfully claimed, "Ginger's a mood booster!" Normally they made jokes whenever Clutch served up his vegan treats. But tonight no one had the energy. Humiliation was exhausting. Even the chocolate fondue fountain, which Clutch had custom built for his only daughter, sat ominously untouched, a reminder of happier times.

Becks reached into her pocket and realized the

business card from Chad Hutchins was still there. She took it out and left it on the picnic table, a stark reminder of how Ruby, via Ellie, was ruining her life. Becks couldn't wait for Mac to hurry up and make them all feel better. It was almost midnight, and still no Mac. She kept checking the security monitors in the kitchen to see if the Prius had pulled in front of the garage.

"Girls, why the long faces?" Clutch sauntered back into the kitchen in his khaki shorts and Tommy Bahama luau shirt. At thirty-nine, Clutch Becks was tall and rangy and still looked and acted like a teenager. "You've had the smoothies and you *still* look bummed? This must be serious." He poured himself his own special smoothie concoction from a pitcher. Becks wrinkled her nose. He was on day two of the total body cleanse, which meant he didn't eat any solid foods and only drank a bizarre brick-colored beverage. It contained maple syrup, lemon juice, and a dousing of Worcestershire sauce. "Do we have to bust out the S'More Machine? Will that bring back the smiles?" Clutch gave a knowing grin to the girls, clearly hoping for one in return.

Becks stuck her hands in the front pocket of her Maui & Sons sweatshirt and sighed. "It's a long story, Pops," she said, not wanting to get into the saga of Ruby and social chair and Austin.

"Well, let me guess. . . ." Clutch pressed his hands to his tanned temples and pretended to concentrate really hard, like a fortune-teller. He had started taking acting classes with Ivanna Chubbuck, and he was always improvising. "I know!" He opened his twinkling blue eyes. "Global warming!"

Becks shook her head.

"Oh, shoot, thought I had it." Clutch pretended to be bummed out. "Um, give me three guesses. . . ." He resumed his fortune-teller position, then snapped his fingers. "Endangered pandas!"

Emily and Coco giggled for the first time that night.

"Oh, I know! Deforestation, right? That's got to be it!"

Becks groaned. "No, Pops. It's BAMS drama."

"Oh," Clutch said, taking a swig of his smoothie. "Real problems."

Becks rolled her eyes, but still managed to smile for the first time that evening.

"So I guess your old man is too much of a geezer to hear all the good gossip, huh?" He put his hands on his lower back, and spoke in a fake-grandfather voice. "Getting too old for this! Oh, my achin' bones! Too old for the BAMS gossip."

Becks blew a strand of strawberry blond hair out of her eyes. She didn't want her dad to feel left out—it had been just her and him for as long as she could remember—but this was about school drama *and* boy drama. Boys complicated eh-ver-ything. Besides, the last time she'd tried to talk to him about Austin, it had been so awkward that they'd never even finished their conversation.

"Well, speaking of BAMS"—Clutch puffed out his lean

chest—"I've agreed to offer our beach for ExtravaBAMSa this year. I just got off the phone with some girl named Ruby and they're using our backyard for Surffest!"

Emily, Coco, and Becks dropped their jaws.

"Uh-oh," Clutch said, looking like he was seeing a tsunami headed his way. "I take it you girls don't like that. Should I call her back and say no?"

"No, that's cool, Pops," Becks said hastily. She didn't want her dad to feel bad about trying to help. "It's just that I'm not feeling very into Surffest this year."

"Wait a second!" Clutch said, making the time-out sign with his tan hands. "*You* aren't into Surffest? Well, maybe the fact that Austin Holloway is going will change your mind. I figure you never get to see him now that he's in high school, so I made sure to invite him." Clutch winked. "Catch y'all laters, girls," he said, saluting. "Gotta learn my lines. If I'm not off-book, they don't let me come to class!"

The second Clutch's green Crocs had gone around the corner, Becks groaned. She turned to her friends. "Did my dad just try to set me up with Austin?" She leaned into her hands.

Coco and Emily giggled.

Becks shook her head, like a dog shaking water off its fur. "I can't take the embarrassment. There's officially *no way* I want to go to ExtravaBAMSa," she said glumly, imagining Austin drooling over Ellie in her very own backyard.

"Tell me about it," Emily sighed, playing with a button on her red pajama top. "Yesterday Señorita Lumley asked me if I wanted a recommendation for a good therapist." She made a concerned face. "E-mee-lee-ah. We *all* need people to talk to."

Becks smiled at her friend's impression. "At least this will all be over in a week."

"The end can't come fast enough. Look at me!" Coco held out her hands to the group. They were so dry that they had scales and cracks. "The industrial soap is turning me into a reptile!" She stuck out her tongue like a lizard.

"Life sucks," Becks said glumly, reaching for another cookie.

"You want to know how much my life sucks?" Coco stood up, fueled by the injustice. "Today at practice—yes, Haylie made us practice on the weekend—I was so bored that I wrote a freaking song about it."

Coco cleared her throat and snapped her fingers three times, finding her note. Then she closed her eyes and started singing:

I'm a sad, sad water boy
Treat me like I'm a toy
That you throw away

It was part Jonas Brothers, part Ashlee Simpson, and it was *intonse*. Coco's eyes were closed like she was performing to a sold-out Staples Center, her body swaying.

'Cause you don't even care
Enough to say buh-bye—

She was midway through the very soulful *buh-bye,* when Mac barged through the teak door with a huge smile on her face.

She paused for a second to observe Coco's bizarre performance. "So sorry to interrupt," Mac addressed the group. "Good news, bad news. What do you want first?"

"Bad news!" Coco sighed, facing Mac.

"Let's get it over with," Becks agreed.

"I didn't think it could get worse," Emily sighed, pulling her hoodie so far over her head that it practically covered her eyes.

"Ruby's got zero intention of ending this charade." Mac made the zero sign with her fingers. She pointed at Coco. "You're going to be water boy forever. There's no way she's going to help us get our lives back."

Emily and Coco looked at each other desperately.

"That's not fair!" Becks cried. "A deal's a deal!"

"Except when it's not," Coco said. "I actually had a feeling about this, after something Haylie said the other day." She crossed her arms. "Mac, didn't you get this in writing? Even I know that you have to get these things in writing!"

Mac looked down at the slate floor. "I seriously screwed up. When Ruby and I discussed the deal, I thought she'd be true to her word."

"Ruby seriously needs a new hobby," Becks said darkly, reaching for another cookie.

"Yes, she does." Mac stuffed her hands into her Habitual jeans pockets. "Unfortunately, until she gets one, making our lives miserable is it."

Emily looked from Becks to Mac to Coco, scanning their faces as if trying to make some sense of this. She looked as though she was about to cry.

"Wasn't there good news?" Becks asked.

"Yes!" Mac said, her eyes lighting up as she sat down at the picnic table, tapping the corner of Chad's Quiksilver business card on the wood. "The good news is, I know what we need to do." Mac looked from girl to girl. They were each waiting for the plan. "Screw working our way up. We sabotage the Thinner Circle."

"How?" Emily, Becks, and Coco asked in unison.

Mac smiled. "Well, we're assistants. We're so low on the totem pole that nobody even notices what we're doing."

Becks shrugged. "I don't get it."

"We use what we know to embarrass them at ExtravaBAMSa." Mac made the Kimmie Tachman paw. "Think about it: Do you realize the kind of all-access pass we have to the Rubybots' lives? They trust us with their most important stuff. I know where Ruby sleeps.

Kimmie's trusting Emily with her pride and joy, her play—Emily and *a live audience*. Ellie will believe anything Becks tells her about surfing. I mean, seriously, girls. Angelina didn't ask Jen if she could have Brad. We just take what is ours. And fast."

The girls stared at Mac in stunned silence. Emily twirled a strand of her cinnamon brown hair. Becks sipped her smoothie. All this talk of manipulation and strategy was making her feel numb. That wasn't her style. "I don't get what you want us to do," Becks said finally.

"I don't have a specific plan," Mac said. "But I do know that Ruby leaves her phone in front of me all the time. Coco, you see the dance team *every day*. Becks and Emily, I'm sure you know sides of Ellie and Kimmie that no one else gets to see. So even if you don't know exactly what you want to do, it'll come to you. Trust me."

Becks stared at the picnic table, thinking about the sides of Ellie she did get to see. She thought about how Ellie was pretending to like surfing just so that Austin would like her. She thought about how Ellie had lied to the Roxy rep and said that she was a surfer.

Before anyone could say anything, Clutch ambled back into the kitchen. "Hey, Miss Mac!" he said. "Just grabbin' some dinner." He opened the refrigerator and took out a pitcher filled with the cleanse. He pointed one of the drinks at Becks. "Kiddo, if you don't want to do the surf thing, it's no problemo." He hip-closed the refrigerator.

Becks's eyes twinkled wickedly. "No, Pops, you were right. I wouldn't miss next weekend for the world." Becks smiled. "And if it's okay with you, I'm going to bring my new friend Ellie. She's really excited."

The other girls looked at her curiously, sly smiles appearing on everyone's faces for the first time that night.

Clutch looked up from his glass. "I can't keep up with you girls, but that sounds good to me."

Becks smiled too, imagining Ellie embarrassing herself at ExtravaBAMSa, in front of everyone. Thanks to Mac, she knew exactly how to make that happen. For the first time in a while, Becks had hope. Poor little Ellie. She had no idea what she was in for.

CHAPTER TWENTY

emily

◀ Sunday September 13 ▶

11:55 AM Mission: WWMSD

Emily had no idea why she was sitting in the back of the Prius on a Sunday morning, driving down Melrose to Pinkberry. They passed the bright blue Pacific Design Center, and Urth Café, where Emily had had her first power meeting with Mac just two weeks ago, and Elixir, the fancy tea store where she'd rehearsed for her first movie role.

To Emily, Los Angeles still looked like a fantasy, with blue skies, palm trees, and shiny Mercedes-Benzes everywhere. It was hard to believe she lived here. Normally Emily loved looking out the window and seeing the Los Angeles she read about in *Us Weekly*. Today she was just frustrated, feeling like Mac was kidnapping her for some mystery mission.

What she did know:

1. Mac had woken her up in Becks's screening room with a piping hot cappuccino, a vegan

blueberry muffin from Zen Bakery (courtesy of Clutch Becks), and the command "We gotta go. Now."

2. Five minutes later, she, Mac, and Erin were in the car and driving to Pinkberry. Mac and Emily had left Becks's house without even a goodbye, let alone a thank-you. Sure, Clutch probably wouldn't care, but it was rude to leave that way. In Iowa, Emily *always* thanked friends' parents for their hospitality after a sleepover.
3. She now officially hated Erin's flute rock, which was blaring over the Prius speakers. It no longer sounded relaxing. It sounded like pain.

"This is going to be great," Mac said without turning around from the front seat. She was swooshing her eyelashes with black Shu Uemura mascara.

What was going to be great? Pinkberry? The ride? Mac's face with mascara? Emily rubbed her temples.

"Mac, I don't understand what you're doing," Emily said calmly. She appreciated Mac's zeal, but sometimes it was annoying to feel like she was just another one of Mac's accessories.

"You'll find out soon enough," Mac said dismissively.

"I'm really not dressed to go anywhere in L.A. right now," Emily said, remembering how paparazzi had popped up behind a parked car at Fred Segal and snapped her picture. Emily imagined getting photographed in her black and white Harajuku Lovers jammies and her camel-colored Uggs. Her friends from Iowa would pick up *Us Weekly*, wondering if she'd pulled a Britney.

Mac ignored her and popped the tube of mascara into her black quilted Chanel makeup bag. "What you don't realize is that Spazmo is the role of a lifetime."

Emily cringed, wondering how her dreams had downgraded from movie star to Spazmo. Hollywood was quicksand for her self-respect. Plus, there was no way that a school play was the role of a lifetime. She thought back to all the times she'd gone to see her best friend, Paige, perform in school plays back in Cedartown and there were *maybe* twenty-five people in the audience, six of them from Paige's family.

"Hank Myler is going to be at that show," Mac said matter-of-factly, referring to the famous director who was known for his quirky independent movies. "His daughter is Minka. Seventh grade. Braces. Freckles. Cute girl. Wears a lot of Anthropologie." Mac rattled off the facts like an FBI agent reciting someone's profile. "She's in the A Capella Club; they're going up before *Judgers & Haters*, so he'll definitely stay for the show." She reached into the glove compartment and pulled out a Red Bull.

"Anyway, Hank is currently attached to *If You Say So*. It's a great script, a comedy about a girl who wakes up at

Disneyland with no memory whatsoever. All she has is her cell phone, and she has to piece together her life through her text messages." Mac smiled like that explained everything. "And the good news is that he's really into casting kids from BAMS, 'cause he went here."

Emily's lips twitched. It had never occurred to her that there was anything good about being in *Judgers & Haters*. She'd been too busy *judging* and *hating* it.

"So what you're saying is that this can be a good role for me?" Emily spoke very slowly, making sure she and Mac were on the same page.

Mac nodded, just as slowly. "Yeah, Spazmo, that's exactly what I'm saying."

"But that doesn't mean Hank is going to want to cast me," Emily pointed out.

"Babe. Everyone who's seen you act has loved you. There are casting directors in this town who you've never even *met* who have you on their radar."

Emily looked out the window and realized they were passing Fred Segal, the most famous boutique in Los Angeles. She smiled, remembering the last time they'd gone on a shopping spree at that store. No such luck today.

Emily leaned back in her seat, feeling flattered. Sometimes she forgot Mac had real reasons for investing so much time in her acting career. Hearing that real Hollywood casting directors were tracking her made Emily feel proud and nervous at the same time.

"'Cause when Hank Myler sees you stealing the show—bravo!" Mac snapped her fingers and pointed at Emily. "You've just managed to give yourself what every actress in this town wants, and that's a chance to audition for Hank Myler."

"It's true," Erin said, speaking up for the first time that car ride. Erin angled the rearview mirror so that she could stare back at Emily. Emily had forgotten she was there. "I had a friend who switched agents just because the new one could get her an audition with Hank."

"Yeah, but Kimmie already took the adorable role for herself," Emily complained.

Mac turned around, leaning over the Prius seat. "That's why I feel bad for Kimmie sometimes. She misses the obvious." Mac snapped the mirror shut. "You're going to *upstage* her."

Emily thought about this, but she still wasn't convinced. "Who's going to want to cast a Spazmo when she's standing next to—"

"Listen," Mac interrupted, "you still have to knock it out of the park. But it's a degree-of-difficulty thing. You're doing a triple lutz and she's just skating. You're the Sasha Cohen here." Emily looked out the car window as they passed a Coffee Bean & Tea Leaf. She was tired of Mac's schemes and surprises. Then again, she couldn't think of any better options. Besides moving home to Iowa.

"Think about it, Ems," Mac began in a persuasive voice, reminding Emily of Adrienne. "How do pretty actresses get noticed?" Without waiting for Emily's response, Mac answered her own question. "They make themselves really *ugly.*"

"Jessica Alba's never ugly," Erin pointed out. "Neither are Jessica Biel or Drew—"

"Duh. I'm not talking about in real life," Mac snapped. "I mean Oscar roles. Take Charlize Theron in *Monster*. Gaining twenty pounds—ew. Ugly makeup, double ew. But she got major Oscar buzz from the moment people saw her transformation. Nicole Kidman with the big fake nose and crazy behavior in *The Hours?* Until they went ugly, all those gals were just one bad review away from *Dancing with the Stars.*"

Emily nodded. She had seen all those movies, and remembered how the actors had transformed their looks. "But I'm not trying to win an Oscar!" Emily protested, throwing her hands in the air. "I'm just trying to break into the business."

Mac looked at her seriously. "That's exactly how you get into the business."

Emily froze and she felt an insta-calm come over her, because she knew Mac was right. For the first time since she'd been sentenced to star in *Judgers & Haters,* there was something about Spazmo that seemed not *I want to cry* awful. As Emily spotted the familiar "Melrose" street sign out the window, she remembered she was in a car being driven on a mystery mission. "Okay. So what does all this have to do with Pinkberry?"

Mac smiled as though she'd been waiting for Emily to ask this very question the whole ride. "From now on, before you do anything, I want you to ask yourself, WWMSD? What would Meryl Streep do?"

"I don't know what Meryl Streep would do," Emily said, confused. Sometimes she thought Mac—like the rest of Bel-Air—was just crazy.

"She'd go to Pinkberry and study a real-life version of Spazmo!" Mac exclaimed. "Remember the Freakberry girl who showed up at Coco's last weekend? Meryl Streep would take note of her mannerisms, her posture, her smile, everything. She'd study the original Spazmo like it was for a final exam," Mac said triumphantly. "I want you to treat this play like it's *The Hours*." Mac smiled. "Now you go find that dorky delivery girl. It's time to turn on your Spazmojo."

Emily smiled as she climbed out of the car and closed the Prius door. She took a deep breath and walked into the green and white store. There, behind the crisp white counter, was the Freakasaurus delivery girl with the stringy dyed purple hair, her shoulders hunched nervously as she took people's frozen yogurt orders. Emily watched her work, awkwardly greeting each customer as though she were about to be yelled at. When Emily got to the front of the line, a slow smile spread across the girl's face.

"I've seen you before!" she squealed, waving her arms and knocking over all the cups in the process.

"I came by to say hi!" Emily said sweetly. "We should hang out."

The Pinkberry girl bent down to pick up the cups, which she promptly dropped all over the floor again the second she put them on the counter. Emily smiled at the girl's awkward mannerisms, realizing this was all material she could use as Spazmo.

Emily leaned over to help, intentionally knocking over more cups. The Freaskasaurus laughed at Emily's "clumsiness," but her laugh sounded more like one high-pitched scream. Emily laugh-yelled back. "You're outta control!" Freakasaurus howled. Her back was bent like a hunchback, and she shook her head with her mouth wide open when she laughed.

"I know!" Emily gasped, matching her tone and posture. She bent forward over the counter, and she left her mouth a little open, as if it was easier than opening and closing it to talk and breathe.

Emily could feel the people in line behind her boring holes into her back with their eyes, waiting to get their fro-yos. But to her surprise, as embarrassing as it was to unleash her inner Spazmo, it was actually a little fun. Out of the corner of her eye, she caught a glimpse of Mac and Erin, watching her from the other side of the store and laughing. For once, Erin wasn't the freakiest person in the room.

And that was exactly the plan.

CHAPTER TWENTY-ONE

COCO

◀ Tuesday September 15 ▶

11:45 AM Dance practice—figure out how to put Mission STTC (Sabotage The Thinner Circle) into effect

Coco hunched in the corner of the dance studio, scrubbing the golden-colored wood floors, while the girls practiced their routine. They were now wearing their costumes: starchy A-line dresses that made them look like umbrellas. A fun idea in theory, but really, who wanted to look like an umbrella?

As the girls barrel-turned, and Coco caught glimpses of their faces, she could tell that they were despondent. Coco knew that she could help save their performance if she could just get some alone time. It was painful, like watching someone walk around with toilet paper stuck to their pants. Just a quick tweak or two (or four) to the routine, and they'd be humiliation-free. She had tried to corner the Bam-Bams at school, but they traveled in a pack, and Haylie was always there, guarding them.

Coco put her hands on the floor and stretched out her back in child's pose. She hadn't known her arms (or her back, or her head, for that matter) could hurt so much from scrubbing. Then again, until becoming the water *boy*, Coco had never scrubbed anything. Her tracksuit was splotched in soapy water and chlorine, and her skin was dry.

Rihanna's "Umbrella" blared, and Coco watched as the Bam-Bams moved through the motions like they were on cruise control. Each time Lucia and Maribel flew past Coco, she noticed how glum and not-smiley they were. When the music finally stopped, Coco looked at the Bam-Bams. They didn't look like the adorable semi-professional team that prompted dance requests from the White House. They looked embarrassed.

"I really think we should cut out that last pirouette," Maribel said.

"That's a great idea," Haylie snapped, "but unfortunately Ruby already approved the dance we have for ExtravaBAMSa. We can't change it this late in the game."

"It's just that—" Maribel stammered.

"You do like performing, right?" Haylie cut her off.

A hush fell over the room as the team realized Haylie was threatening Maribel. But what could anyone say? Haylie was right. The dance had been approved. Only she could petition to change it at this point. And even though it wasn't working, she didn't seem inclined to try to fix it, since that would be tantamount to admitting her own incompetence.

"You're right," Maribel said, looking at her water

bottle. She turned it upside down and stared glumly at the bottom.

If only she could show them how to defeat Haylie, Coco thought desperately. If only she could find a way to get them alone. And then she had an idea.

When the girls went back to rehearsing, Coco reached for her royal blue Sharpie pen and wrote on the label of each water bottle: *Meet under willow tree AFTER BELL! SECRET DANCE MTG. SHH (Super Hush Hush) Don't tell Haylie!!*

As she put the cap on her pen, she smiled at her own clever plotting.

This must be what it felt like to be Mac.

Three hours later, Coco waited under the willow tree hoping *someone* would show up. It suddenly occurred to her that she'd made a huge mistake. Of course the girls were tired of Haylie and her dance, but that didn't mean they would actually take a secret dance team meeting without her.

Coco put her iPhone into her satchel, getting ready to leave. She looked up just as Maribel and Lucia arrived, with their navy hoodies pulled over their faces, bank robber style.

Then Anais showed up.

Then Taylor.

Soon the entire dance team minus Haylie was there, huddled around the tree, staring at Coco, who felt—even if it was for a few seconds—like she was captain again.

"Okay, listen." Coco cleared her throat. "I've called you here because I see you guys dance every day. I know how great you can be." She looked at the group nervously, hoping no one would take anything personally. "But you're going to embarrass yourselves if you perform this dance."

"Word!" Maribel agreed. "And I voted to do your dance 'cause I loved it."

"Thanks," Coco said calmly. "The problem is, I spent hours making it a good *solo,* not an *ensemble.*"

Taylor and Eden smiled for her to continue, and the rest of the group nodded.

"But it could be worthy of your talents," Coco added. "It just needs a few tweaks so the audience knows where to look."

The girls smiled. Clearly this was the first sensical thing they'd heard in a while.

"What you should be doing is just giving focus to one dancer during the first eight counts. Save the coordinated routines for the chorus," Coco said. "And you . . ." Coco looked right into Eden's icy blue eyes. "You're underused. You should be leading the first solo. You're doing spirals, but they don't work so early in the song. It would be way cooler to throw in some fan kicks in the beginning so you're connecting with the audience. Besides, you can do those in your sleep." Coco snapped her fingers. Eden smiled, as though she had longed for someone to acknowledge that. "We should start with you for a quick energy shot."

Coco looked at the rest of the team, their eyes still focused on her. "There are a lot of barrel turns right now—but that doesn't mean you *all* have to be doing barrel turns." She pointed to Maribel and Lucia. "It's a waste to hide you behind all these tall girls. You two need to be in the center. And *Taylor*." Coco looked right at Taylor White. "You just need to show us that beautiful smile of yours." Coco went through every girl in the group, until the entire team knew exactly what they had to do to step up their routine.

"Oh, and one more thing," Coco said, reaching into her giant zebra-striped bag. "You can't go out dressed like umbrellas." She handed the girls tiny silver shorts with shimmery pale leotards. In the light, they sparkled like rainwater.

Anais gasped. "It's exactly what I envisioned us wearing!" she said as she took the new costume.

"They're perfect," Taylor cried, turning the shorts over like a Christmas present.

"Don't tell Haylie," Coco whispered. "Or she'll go bananas."

"Coco." Maribel looked up at Coco with her big eyes. "I'm so sorry about you being water boy. We've all talked about how this blows. It just seems like there's nothing we can do. Ruby won't allow us to change the dance. And Haylie threatened to drop our blooper reel on the intranet—*and* show it at ExtravaBAMSa, in lieu of our performance—if we do anything against her."

Everyone knew that the Bam-Bams kept a super-secret reel of moves from the girls' auditions, usually showcasing sillier moves and mistakes. Generally it was a way to laugh at how far everyone had come. But no one besides the dance team was supposed to see it.

Coco flinched at the idea that Haylie had threatened to make their audition tapes public. This was more than just power going to her head—this was full-on treachery. Coco couldn't believe how much she'd underestimated Ruby and Haylie's ruthlessness.

Maribel was still talking animatedly, excited to get this off her chest. "And I can't deal with that before ExtravaBAMSa," She pointed to her twin sister, Lucia. "We have relatives flying in from Chicago to see us perform." Lucia nodded solemnly.

"I wish you were captain," Taylor said wistfully.

"It's such a bummer you're the water boy," Anais said, looking at Coco sadly.

"I wish you could do this dance with us," said Eden.

"I know!" Taylor cried.

Coco smiled. "Actually, there is a way. I'll do the new dance with you. We'll leave Haylie onstage, doing her own dance. She'll look stupid in her costume, and she'll have to get out of the way for us."

Maribel blinked, twice, and exchanged glances with

Lucia. Taylor, Ames, and Eden smiled like spies who'd just been given a top-level mission.

"Sounds like a plan!" Maribel said, speaking for the group.

"Well, I'm just so happy to help you all," Coco said, trying to hide how relieved she felt to know that her captainship had not been a one-day joke. "We can practice our routine here next week," she said casually, buzzing with excitement over this new plan.

Coco looked into the sea of faces staring at her respectfully and understood why her mother had emphasized the respect of her peers so much. Earning it was the best feeling in the world. Next week couldn't come fast enough.

CHAPTER TWENTY-TWO

becks

◀ Wednesday September 16 ▶

4:20 PM Teach Ellie to "surf"

7:20 PM Sunset? What time is sunset? Why does it have to be so late?

Straddling her surfboard in the middle of the Pacific Ocean, Becks closed her eyes and felt the last few rays of sunlight on her face. It was Magic Hour, right before sunset, which meant that the sun was starting to cast its shimmery pink glow over the ocean. Becks and Ellie had spent all afternoon surfing—if you could call it that. It was more like three hours of: yelling instructions at Ellie, one almost-standing-up moment, zero good conversation, and waaaaay too much shivering and not-surfing.

Becks realized an entire afternoon had gone by and she hadn't surfed a single wave. She sighed. What a waste. It was like going to Coffee Bean and getting a water.

"All righty, Becks," Ellie giggled as she straddled her board. She was wearing her black Roxy bikini. "Mama Ellie's gonna do it this time."

She paddled quickly, her skinny arms turning like

wheels in a hamster cage. She got her feet on her board, but then, just as she began to stand up, she crumpled into the wave. Her board bounced back to the ocean, and Ellie bobbed after it, for what felt like the four hundredth time that day.

The only thing good about seeing Ellie mess up was that it meant that Becks's plan was perfectly in action: Ellie was getting just comfortable enough that Becks would be able to embarrass her at Surffest.

"No worries—I'm gonna nail the next one!" Ellie chirped, totally unfazed by her string of failures.

Becks rolled her eyes and looked at her white stucco house in the distance. For the first time ever, she wished she were home instead of on her surfboard. She'd had no idea how cold it could get when you were just sitting in the middle of the ocean and not surfing. Her teeth were chattering.

"I saw that eye roll!" Ellie said teasingly. "Watch me," she commanded. Then, like a windup toy, she paddled her stick-skinny, copper-tan arms in fast circles through the water. Just when Becks expected Ellie to fall, her black bikini popped above the crest. Ellie was standing up! And she was riding the wave all the way to shore!

Becks's heart soared with surprise and pride. "Yeah, Ellie!" Becks screamed. "GO! GO! GO!" Becks watched Ellie ride the wave all the way to the shore before she hopped onto the sand. Ellie waved her arms and did a chicken dance like a football player who had just made a touchdown.

Becks felt a surge of nostalgia, remembering her own excitement the first time she stood up on her board, in Oahu, when she was four. A tiny part of her was jealous that Ellie got to have that thrill, which only happened once in lifetime.

It was unfortunate, because even though she didn't want to, Becks was starting to like Ellie. She was *kind* of fun. And Becks had to give the girl credit: She was obsessed with getting better at surfing. All the times Becks had wanted to duck in early, Ellie had insisted they stay out until she got better in some way. Minus the Rubybot factor, Ellie was close to cool. Becks shrugged away those feelings and quickly paddled to catch a wave so that she could go talk to Ellie on the shore.

"DID YOU SEE ME, BECKS?" Ellie screamed, as Becks dragged her board out of the ocean and onto the white Malibu sand. It was almost dark, and the houses were like shadows on the shore.

"Yeah, that was a start," Becks said casually.

"Um, earth to Becks?" Ellie said, smiling. "Is that all I get? I just stood up on my board!"

"Okay. Good job, you stood up," Becks muttered, feeling a tiny nagging voice in her head saying, *Just say congratulations*. But then she heard someone clapping. She turned around and saw Austin, wearing tattered green cargo shorts and a tight black T-shirt, his brown hair flopping lazily in his blue-gray eyes. "Nice work, Professor Becks! You should teach a class!"

Becks stood taller, beaming with pride. She'd never been called that before. And yet there Austin was, proud of her for having taught someone to do something they both loved. It was the first time she'd felt good around him in a while. She was relieved to know that they could connect as friends, since things had been so awkward following the Pinkberry debacle.

Ellie put her hands on her hips and giggled flirtatiously. "How about some props for the excellent student?" She batted her eyelashes like she'd read a manual on *How to Steal a Guy*.

Austin turned to Ellie. He seemed impressed by her boldness. And then it hit Becks like a ten-foot wave: Austin had said he couldn't like a girl who couldn't surf, and now Ellie could.

I've created a monster.

Ellie smiled, enjoying the attention. "We should all go grab Pinkberry to celebrate!"

The word *Pinkberry* lingered in the air like the stench of sewage at El Segundo Beach.

"Nah, I should get going," Austin said, looking down at the sand before he slunk back to his house.

"'Byee!" Ellie called after him. He didn't turn around.

Becks's cheeks flushed and she remembered all over again why she could never ever be friends with Ellie. Sabotage was game on.

Becks turned to Ellie and smiled. "That was seriously great!" she said in her happiest fake voice. "But if you really want to impress the folks at Surffest, we should learn one more move."

Ellie smiled at Becks, as if deciding whether or not to take the plunge. "Okay," she said finally, tugging at the black straps of her bikini. "Sweet."

The girls paddled back into the chilly ocean. "Watch me," Becks said. And then that nagging voice in her head got a lot louder, practically shouting, *This is really not cool.* Becks paddled away the doubt. She stood on her board and then crept her way forward until her toes were hanging off the end. The move was called Toes on the Nose, and she'd learned it a few years earlier at surf camp in Malibu. It was definitely not a novice move.

"That looks hard," Ellie said cautiously when Becks paddled back to meet her.

"It's really not," Becks insisted. It wasn't a total lie, since what Becks meant was, *It's really not that hard for me.* But it had taken her nine years and a lot of practice.

"All righty, Becksy, I trust you," Ellie said.

"Yeah," Becks said. "Think how surprised Austin will be when you rip it up at Surffest."

Ellie smiled, as if imagining herself zigzagging across the waves like a girl version of Kelly Slater. "Speaking of, it's just a friends thing between you guys, right?"

Becks's pulse raced. She *never* discussed her crushes with anyone outside the Inner Circle. Though it was nice of Ellie even to bring it up, like she was asking permission to go for Austin. But then Becks realized: Ellie had seen the Slumbergate video, which meant she knew Becks had a crush. She wasn't trying to be buddy-buddy, and she wasn't being considerate. She was rubbing it in.

"We're just friends." Becks gritted her teeth.

"Good, 'cause I think it's only a matter of time before he's mine," Ellie said confidently. Before Becks could respond, Ellie paddled back out to catch a wave. Becks watched her from her board. Ellie managed to stand up again, but before she could even begin to move forward on the board, she wiped out, tumbling into the ocean awkwardly while her board bobbed to shore.

If she couldn't even stay standing, there was no way this girl could get Toes on the Nose in time for the surf exhibit. She'd look like a terrible surfer and make a fool of herself in front of everyone. And it was Ellie's turn to find out how that felt.

It was almost too easy.

CHAPTER TWENTY-THREE

mac

◄ Thursday September 17 ►

4 PM Spinning for 45 minutes to burn negative energy

6 PM Ruby thing @ Bristol Farms

9 PM Post-Ruby steam room/toxins flush

"Today's going to be really easy," Ruby said from the entrance of Bristol Farms on the corner of Doheny. It was a high-end grocery store in Beverly Hills that looked like a colonial mansion with a white arch entryway surrounded by bright green plants. The parking lot was filled with Audis, Mercedes-Benzes, and Lexuses, and it catered to young starlets and the paparazzi. It was exactly where Mac did *not* want to be, because she wanted to be done with PDA (Public Displays of Assistantship).

"I just need you to push the shopping cart and grab the items I tell you to grab," Ruby said, leaning on her crutches as they stepped into the store, passing a perfectly coiffed Scarlett Johansson clutching a canvas grocery bag on her way out.

Mac hoped that if she smiled and chatted with Ruby it would look like two friends going shopping together instead of an assistant on duty with her boss. Mac felt even more embarrassed, because she was still honoring the deal to not wear anything Ruby owned. Which meant that Mac was left to wear her Vanessa Bruno jumpsuit, way too glam for grocery shopping. Ruby was wearing the same James Perse tee that Mac had worn days earlier with the Paige jeans. Which meant the look was already over.

They passed the cheese aisle, and Mac inhaled the aroma of freshly grated parmesan. Ruby would not stop talking. "I really want your help with the finale 'cause I need it to go off without a hitch. I'm doing my ode to BAMS, to determine if we should release it as my first single from my new album," Ruby said, seriously. "Does that make sense?"

Mac paused thoughtfully. Even if it was Ruby, there was something about giving people career advice that gave her a buzz. "Yeah. The song is about BAMS, so you know the audience will like the content at the very least. If they like the melody, then you know it's worth it to debut it in front of a bigger, non-BAMS market and see how it flies." Mac shrugged. It seemed like common-sense PR work. (As long as Mac ignored the fact that Ruby was using a benefit for the Third World to promote herself.)

"Oooh, you are so smart!" Ruby squealed. "That's exactly what Brigham says." She made a concerned face. "He wants me to lip-synch the one we recorded."

Mac smiled. Jackpot! *This* was information she could use. Mac carefully filed that tidbit away in the

"Operation Take Down Ruby" part of her brain and quickly slapped a smile on her face to uphold her façade. "Well, that makes sense," Mac said, squeezing the shopping cart handle so she wouldn't sound overexcited at the turn this conversation was taking. "If it's a debut, you want to make sure it lands just right. You don't want to take any chances with a live performance."

Ruby looked relieved. She stared at Mac seriously, her violet eyes focused like high beams.

"I'm so glad we're finally friends." Ruby smiled.

Mac felt a jolt inside her body, but somehow managed to smile back, numb from shock. Did Ruby not know the meaning of the word *friend*? Did she not know that friends didn't make friends push grocery carts?

"Oooh, Roquefort samples!" Ruby exclaimed, eyeing the dairy section, where they had laid out mini bites of the stinky French cheese. "I want some!"

Mac shivered—she was very anti–free food. Her mother had instilled in her the fear of germs and of being seen standing up and grazing.

Ruby darted off, leaving Mac all alone with the cart and her black quilted Chanel bag. Mac spotted Ruby's iPhone poking out of the front pocket. Her heart skipped a beat as she eyed the shiny device. Another Damage Potential opp. And this time, Mac was going to take it.

Mac was about to grab the phone like a South Beach dieter devouring white bread when she realized—it looked . . . different. The iPhone was a tiny bit too wide. It was Swarovski studded.

And totally fake.

Phone clone!

Mac yanked her hand away from the fake phone as though the instrument had been dipped in high-fructose corn syrup. Suddenly the dots connected like a Seurat painting: *Ruby had been trying to trick her all along!* All those opportunities that Mac had passed up to snoop hadn't been coincidences. They'd been *traps.*

Mac's mind quickly scrolled through a mental slide show:

1. Origami bird in the Deener jeans in Ruby's closet
2. Computer ping, ping, pinging in Ruby's bedroom
3. Phone left out at the Getty kitchen
4. Presently: phone clone

Mac smiled, pleased that she was worth so much mental energy and even more pleased that she hadn't fallen for it. She tried to turn the cart toward the rows of condiments, but Ruby was blocking the route, pointing her right crutch at Mac. "Busted! Phone snoop!"

Mac calmly looked up. "Huh?" she said innocently.

Ruby eyed Mac up and down, resting her eyes on Mac's hands, which were very clearly curled around the cart handle. Then Ruby slowly slid her gaze to the dummy phone, which was very clearly *not* in Mac's hands.

"Oops!" Ruby said, staring off at the row of gourmet nut butters. She actually blushed. "I thought—"

Mac shrugged. "I respect your privacy."

There was a long pause.

"Well, good." Ruby swept her feathered bangs out of her face. "That was a test to see if I could trust you. And you passed." Ruby pantomimed clapping. "Now you can *really* help me with the finale. I need your impeccable taste to decide which napkin design to go with."

"Whatever you say, boss," Mac said, amazed that she'd gone from enemy to frenemy in one-point-five grocery store aisles. Ruby was finally going to give her some real responsibilities, which she'd promptly abuse. It was all working out better than she had planned.

"I'm also going to need to run my speech by you," Ruby said bossily. "I need to strike the proper tone—you know, classy but young like me? And we need to pick a color scheme." Ruby leaned on her right crutch, as if she were stopping to think. "Maybe after we take care of all this social chair business, you could come to my next sleepover?" She smiled. "But, like, *not* as the butler—as my guest?"

Mac smiled fake-shyly, hoping to seem truly touched by Ruby's not-really-big gesture. Even if her smile was phony, Mac's happiness was genuine: She was *in*. And she was going to make sure that by the time Extrava-BAMSa was over, Ruby was way, way *out*.

CHAPTER TWENTY-FOUR

becks

◀ Saturday September 19 ▶

11 AM ExtravaBAMSa kickoff in Malibu

12 PM Surf-off

2 PM Celebrate with Austin at BBQ?

Coco, Becks, and Mac were standing on Becks's beach, holding a private conference in the middle of Surffest.

"Ruby completely thinks I'm her BFF," Mac said proudly, retying the string on her pastel pink Chloé halter dress, which she'd borrowed from Coco because of Ruby's no-dupes rule. "She told me everything she plans to do for ExtravaBAMSa—it's like she's giving me the handbook on how to sabotage her. Only nine more hours till we get our lives back," Mac said excitedly.

"And the Bam-Bams have their new costumes," Coco said, dabbing La Prairie sunscreen around her eyes. "I can't wait until tonight." She grinned wickedly.

Becks smiled at Coco, who was not usually so scheming or so adventurous. It was funny to see how Pax Rubana was bringing out new sides of her friends. She shoved her hands into the pockets of her baby blue sweatshirt—her muscles couldn't get cold while she waited to surf.

"And Spazmo's a green light," Emily said proudly, showing off her newly dyed crimson hair, à la Spazmo. "I am officially all over this role. Me and Freakberry are like this." She crossed her fingers.

Across the beach, Becks spotted Ruby and the Ruby-bots all wearing the same Gucci sunglasses—the ones Mac had worn up until they'd copied her. They looked like Guccibots. They were all staring curiously at the Inner Circle, as if waiting to see what they would do next. Even as social pariahs, the I.C. were still the ones to watch.

Becks barely recognized her backyard. The normally serene beach had been completely transformed for Surf-fest: Bleachers had been built just for the day; royal blue tents had been set up by sponsors Roxy and Gatorade; and there was a giant tower by the bleachers, so a camera crew could televise the event. Kelly Slater, the world champion surfer (and an old buddy of Clutch's) was piling strawberries and grapes onto a black plastic plate in the VIP breakfast tent, which had been catered by Marmalade Cafe. He chucked a grape at Laird Hamilton, another world-famous surfer.

Surffest looked like a VIP party for X Games, which Becks had been to several times with her father. Besides Kelly Slater and Laird Hamilton, Trent Munro and Shaun White were there. Kate Hudson and Goldie Hawn had brought their beach chairs.

In front of the packed bleachers, Becks spied Austin

and Mac's brother, Jenner, tossing a football on the sand with some other guys from Bel-Air Prep. Even the alterna-kids had decided to show up—they were sitting in the back row, holding books and pretending to read.

Becks glanced back to the ocean, where the waves were a mess of choppy whitewash. Just then the voice of Vivian Kelley, BAMS's athletic director, boomed over the speaker system. "Attention, BAMS community! Welcome to our annual Surffest, where all the money from your admission ticket goes to Save Darfur!"

That was Becks's cue to make her way toward the water, since she was up first. The day was kind of like a surfing competition, in that there were heats, and everyone got to surf one wave. But unlike most surf competitions, which were only open to surf team members, Surffest was open to the whole school and anyone who wanted to give it a shot (hence: Ellie). To give the day a competitive edge, there were trophies for joke awards. In earlier years, Becks had won Most Unusual Wipeout (for a failed jump off her longboard) and Most Creative (for a handstand on her longboard).

Vivian continued with her intro speech. "Today we are going to begin with our very own star surfer, Evangelina Becks, and then we'll wrap it up with a surf exhibit by our newbies. As a reminder, the price of your ticket will be donated to Save Darfur, but anything you want to give beyond that will be happily accepted. First off, ladies and gentlemen, I give you Evangelina Becks!"

Becks smiled when she heard her name called. Normally she got jittery in a good way when it was time to surf in front of crowds, but her confidence was so high from having surfed the Pipeline in Hawaii this summer that Malibu seemed fun and easy by comparison.

She waved to the crowd and darted into the water, holding her board under her right arm. As she glided into the ocean on her board, she dug her arms into the water after a swell. The water was surprisingly choppy, even by non-Malibu standards, Becks realized, when she rode her first few waves to shore. It was the kind of surf she loved—big and pounding, and it made her surfing look extra impressive, because she could fly down the line gracefully and quickly. The crowd roared with applause when Becks turned her board and then did a cross-step as she walked across it.

When she finished, even though her ears were filled with salt water, Becks could hear everyone cheering for her. She made her way to shore (discreetly wedgie-checking herself before she got too close to the spectators) and then took a bow. A huge grin spread across her face when she spotted Mac, Coco, and Emily jumping up and down, waving homemade BECKS signs like she was a rock star. But then, remembering why her surfing had been so impressive, she freaked: Those waves were rough! The beginners were up next, and Ellie couldn't be in that water. She rushed over to the tarp where the newer surfers were waiting.

"Ellie, I need to tell you something!" Becks said in a rush.

"Becks! What's up?" Ellie stuck up her tiny hand for a high five. She was wearing the same black Roxy bikini that had become her surfing uniform, and her long blond hair was in a French braid down her back. Becks imagined Ellie trying Toes on the Nose, and all Becks could see was Ellie's teeny self getting knocked by her board. She winced. No matter how jealous Becks might have been, she didn't want Ellie to get hurt.

Becks grabbed Ellie's hand instead of high-fiving, to show this was serious. "Listen, you know that move I showed you? Please promise me you won't try it. The waves are just too big today."

"Little Miss Worry Pants, I'll be fine." Ellie patted her straw blond braid and smiled. Then she grabbed her board, turned, and took long strides toward the water. Becks chased after her, feeling very much like Austin's dog, Boone, desperate for some attention. Soon they were close to the water, out of earshot of the crowd.

"No, seriously, Ellie, the waves are too big," Becks called after her. "It was a really calm day when we practiced." By then they were both standing ankle-deep in the Pacific Ocean. To anyone else, it looked like a coach talking to her athlete.

"So I wipe out?" Ellie giggled. "It'll be impressive that I even tried. No one expects me to be as good as you . . . *yet*," Ellie said. She shot a coy glance over at

Austin, who was still tossing a football with Jenner. Ellie's gaze returned to Becks. "Is this about *him*?" Ellie cocked her eyebrow in Austin's direction.

"No, Ellie, I *swear* this isn't about Austin," Becks said desperately.

Vivian Kelley's voice boomed over the speaker system. "All right, next up, our new surfers will have five minutes to tear up a wave for your enjoyment. So please put your hands together for our novices!"

Becks and Ellie shared a shimmering glare. "You don't have to be jealous, okay?" Ellie said as she ran into the water with the other four surfers.

"But that's not it—" Becks cried out, but it was useless. Ellie was paddling into the waves, and the warning was drowned out by the surf.

Becks looked down at her G-Shock watch. Five minutes couldn't be over fast enough. A lot could happen in that time. She watched as Ellie paddled out and let a few swells pass her by. Then, when a big wave started to sweep toward the shore, Ellie ducked in. Becks winced, knowing it was too big. Ellie paddled her arms and put her foot out to stand on the board.

Becks anxiously squeezed her fingers inside her sweatshirt. She watched as Ellie stood up on her board. Ellie's balance was shaky, but she was up there for several seconds, long enough for Becks to see a huge smile on her face. A tiny part of Becks lit up, knowing that she had taught Ellie how to do that. The crowd roared for Ellie.

Kelly Slater let out a whoop. Austin cupped his hands around his mouth and screamed, "GO, ELLIE!"

And then, Becks's life went into blurry slow motion, as if she'd tumbled underwater. Ellie took baby steps over to the edge of the board. She raised her arms out to wave to the crowd, a proud smile spreading across her face. She took a tiny step toward the nose of the board. Then, as quickly as she'd stood, Ellie's board plunged down and kicked high up into the air. Ellie plummeted headfirst into the water. The waves rolled forward, and Ellie's board zoomed to the sand. But there was no sign of Ellie.

Becks gasped.

For seconds, all Becks saw was more surf churning to shore. A group of people ran to the waves to watch out for Ellie. She was totally MIA. Becks ran to the front of the beach, waiting for Ellie's head to resurface.

Austin charged into the water, *Baywatch* style, reaching his arms to the sides, checking for her body. Becks's mind was thrashing with scenarios: Ellie was unconscious or cut up by the fins of her board. Or both. Or worse . . .

Finally, Austin pulled a listless body from the surf. He carried Ellie fireman style over his shoulder back to the shore and set her down carefully, as though she were a porcelain doll. Becks charged over to them, fearing the worst. She looked down at Ellie, who was sputtering water. Austin wiped her face while he held her head.

"What just happened?" Ellie said dazedly. Becks breathed a sigh of relief.

Austin looked into her eyes. "Ellie, were you trying Toes on the Nose? Why did you ever think you could do that? It's way too advanced."

Ellie looked over at Becks, a swell of understanding washing over her face. She smiled knowingly. Finally, she looked right at Austin. "Becks taught me."

Austin's blue-gray eyes flashed with disappointment. "Becks taught you *that*?"

Becks's heart sank. She wished she could bury herself underground like a sand crab. Her face flushed bright red, but she couldn't think of how to explain herself in a way that would make sense.

"I wanted to impress you," Ellie said simply, looking right into Austin's eyes.

"You don't need to do that to impress me," Austin said tenderly. He squeezed Ellie's hand and stared at Becks with his blue-gray eyes. His look was one of disgust and surprise.

"I guess you just never know what people are thinking," Austin said gently to Ellie, his gaze still locked on Becks. In the thirteen years Becks had known Austin Holloway, she'd never seen him look at her like that.

CHAPTER TWENTY-FIVE

COCO

◄ Saturday September 19 ►

6:45 PM Time to make Bam-Bams history!

Five minutes before the Bam-Bams were slated to perform, Coco hid backstage in the wings, arranging the water bottles in alphabetical order, pretending to still be in water boy mode. Inside, she was tingling with excitement at the sounds coming from the auditorium. The sold-out crowd was buzzing. Coco imagined future Bam-Bams discussing the night: . . . *And then Coco Kingsley took the stage, overthrew the evil empire, and restored glory to our team.*

The Bam-Bams had arranged for a smoke machine to blow a giant puff of smoke, covering the entire stage, which dovetailed perfectly with Coco's plan. It was supposed to go like this:

1. House lights dim.
2. Girls charge the stage in their first position.
3. Smoke covers the stage (Coco sneaks into this lineup).

4. Chords start.
5. Lights pop on.
6. Dance begins.
7. Haylie realizes she's wearing old costume and doing the wrong dance.
8. Haylie looks like a total fool and leaves the stage.
9. Coco dances flawlessly, steals the show, impressing Mom, Dad, and BAMS.

Easy.

The smoke machine, which had been Haylie's one good idea, was a total gift. All she had to do was run out in the first second of smoke and she'd be totally undiscoverable. From her hours of watching dress rehearsals, Coco knew exactly how to time it. The girls would do the new dance, and Coco would be their leader. Haylie would look left out and stupid.

Coco peered into the crowd, looking down upon the sea of faces. She quickly spotted her mother, in the third row from the center, wearing a yellow 3.1 Phillip Lim minidress. Even in a sea of people, Cardammon popped. Next to her, Charles Kingsley was wearing a navy suit with an ascot. Coco beamed, proud that her father had taken the time to dress up for this event. Clearly it meant a lot to him. In the front row, she saw Mac and Becks sitting together, looking as excited for her as she felt. She knew Emily was somewhere backstage, preparing for her Spazmo performance and sending Coco good vibes.

The Bam-Bams came together for a team hug, wearing their starchy A-line dresses that made them look like umbrellas, bathing caps hiding their hair. Coco's shiny dark mane was pulled back, held tight with six bobby pins and hair spray. Her skin was shimmered with extra powder—enough to make her look natural to a crowd of hundreds of people. She unzipped her water boy jacket and untied the cord to her pants, making sure she could fling them off. Underneath was her shiny leotard, designed to glimmer like raindrops. She hoped the Bam-Bams had figured out how to snap off their umbrella dresses. That was the one thing she'd forgotten to have them practice during their secret dance sessions. Coco eyed the green room to find a way to secretly check with Lucia or Maribel, but they were still caught up in the group hug, with Haylie at the center.

But just then Vivian Kelley's voice blared in surround sound. She was speaking in an announcer-y voice, like she was Ryan Seacrest. "Lay-dies and gentlemen, tonight we bring you the most celebrated dance team in Los Angeles, the Bam-Bams!"

The girls broke apart from their hug, patting each other on the back, and then rushed to the wings. Maribel stood right next to Coco.

"You ready?" Coco whispered.

Maribel's eyes stayed focused on the stage. She said

something under her breath that Coco couldn't understand.

Vivian continued her speech: "The Bam-Bams have performed in five countries and thirteen states, two Super Bowls, and at the White House." The crowd roared. Someone yelled out, "ROCK IT, MARIBEL! GO, LUCIA!" The lights dimmed to a blue glow. "You know them, you love them. . . ."

"GOOOOO, GIRLS!" Haylie hiss-whispered to the group.

"Please put your hands together for Bel-Air Middle School's dance team, the one and only Bam-Bams!"

The girls ran onstage to take their positions, heads down, hands clasped, index fingers pointing to the ceiling. As the smoke hissed, billowing over the stage, Coco flung off her tracksuit and leapt out from backstage. Hidden in the smoke clouds, she quietly assumed her place in front of the Bam-Bams, fingers clasped and pointing at the ceiling.

The opening beats of "Umbrella" started, and the lights popped on. The Bam-Bams were off! Coco landed her double pirouette perfectly. Then, just as she'd done by the tree, she nailed her first eight-count, feeling alive with each step. She leaned down into her right leg and leapt up, going for a barrel turn.

And then it happened.

Thud.

She crash-landed.

Did someone put a pole onstage?

Coco looked up and realized . . . that "pole" was Haylie Fowler. Their eyes locked for a millisecond, before Haylie went right back to dancing the old routine, which was exactly what all the other girls were dancing. Lucia did the exact same spiral as Maribel, who did the exact same spiral as Taylor. They were all wearing their very coordinated umbrella outfits. Coco looked like a total outcast, sitting gracelessly on her bum in a mismatched outfit while the girls danced around her. She felt like a piece of left-on-the-street Ikea furniture.

Between spins, Haylie leaned in and whispered to Coco, "Next time you double-cross me, don't tell a group of girls who like shopping at the Grove."

So Haylie had found out and turned the tables on Coco at the last minute. Coco couldn't believe that she was the one sitting shamefully in front of a full auditorium, suffering the fate she'd so carefully planned for Haylie. Coco looked into the packed audience. She slid backward like a crab toward the wings, sweeping away the dust and the remnants of her dignity.

As she slowly pushed her way offstage, Coco got an excruciating final look at her friends. Mac's jaw was wide open, and Becks was wincing as though someone was giving her Indian burns. As Coco scanned the faces of strangers around them, she saw what she'd known she'd see: Everyone was looking at her like she was a total freak. She had never felt so ugly or embarrassed.

And then, just when Coco thought it was not humanly possible to feel worse, she spotted Cardammon and her father. The horror on their super-tanned faces said it all. Coco had gone from fairy tale to cautionary tale in exactly two eight-counts.

CHAPTER TWENTY-SIX

emily

◄ Saturday September 19 ►

8 PM My L.A. acting debut (yay!) in *Judgers & Haters*. WWPFD: What Would Pinkberry Freak Do? Channel her to the max

8:30 PM Mission: Meet Hank Myler!

Emily stood in the green room at 7:57 p.m., playing with her long strands of hair while her legs trembled underneath her. She had raced here seconds after seeing Coco's failed coup, and it had only made her more nervous that maybe the plan wouldn't work as Mac had promised.

Emily had spent the past week shadowing the Pinkberry girl, whose real name was Suzie Dooley. She'd learned how to dye her hair that horrific color (cranberry juice or Kool-Aid), where to buy vests (Crossroads or Goodwill, never spend more than five dollars), and why the *Battlestar Galactica* pins all over the vests (they were conversation starters!).

She was seconds away from her Los Angeles acting debut, even if it was *Judgers & Haters*.

Emily had started to walk with her shoulders more scrunched, like someone had just asked her a question about photosynthesis or something else she just couldn't answer off the top of her head. Just holding her body that way made Emily feel like a more nervous person, as if an asteroid was going to crash to earth any second. She'd even started reading *National Geographic* before going to bed, just because Suzie said it was part of her nightly routine.

On the bright side: Emily knew that her acting was getting better, because everyone at BAMS thought she really was Spazmo. The downside, of course, was that everyone at BAMS thought she really was Spazmo.

Emily nervously tapped at her headgear, feeling the ping inside her mouth and head. About four rehearsals ago she'd gotten over the fact that she was wearing used (but sterilized) headgear. Now it almost made her laugh. Except that her palms were sweaty and her right leg was clattering nervously. Emily was anxious for that familiar *click*—that moment when her personality disappeared and the *character* took over.

The green room, where actors relaxed before performances, was really painted red, and it was lined with black velvet couches and ottomans. In the middle there was a flat table with bowls of mini Jolly Ranchers, M&M's, and Jelly Bellies. Emily sat on a black couch and reached for a Mountain Dew. She steered the straw through the wire-trap maze of her headgear to take a sugar-boosting swig. Kimmie stood in the middle of the room, stretching herself up one vertebrae at a time, muttering, "The rain in Spain stays mainly on the plain," the last of her warm-ups for her body and voice. When she'd rolled her head to a standing-straight position, Kimmie walked over to Emily. "How's my favorite Spazmo?"

The real answer was that Emily was thinking about how much she hated the play and looking so ugly, and just wanted to knock it out of the park so that Hank Myler would notice her—but of course she couldn't say any of *that*, so she just shrugged.

Kimmie smiled and gave her a thumbs-up sign. "Break a leg, Spazzy!"

Before Emily could respond, the lights dimmed and the audience began clapping. And then, as if by magic, Emily clicked into Spazmode.

She barged onto the stage, totally oblivious to the crowd. "Knock, knock—who's at my door? I'm Thpathmo and I want to know," she said, slamming the door to her stage bedroom. And then, to her great surprise—because that wasn't even the joke—the audience actually *laughed.* "I mean theriously!" Emily-as-Spazmo moaned. She didn't feel self-conscious. In fact, her lines came louder and clearer, and she forgot to think about how stupid the play was. She was just thinking like Spazmo: Someone was at her door, and she wanted to know who it was.

Emily barely noticed one of Elliot Tachman's assistants videotaping the performance in the front row next to Elliot himself. And she definitely didn't see Adrienne or Becks or Mac smiling with her because she was so engrossed in responding to Kimmie's character, who at that moment was standing in her stage doorway, looking lost.

The stage was set up to look like a girl's bedroom, which in Kimmie's mind meant pink everywhere. There was pink wallpaper, a pink futon, and a pink refrigerator. Emily slunk onto the futon while Kimmie's character recited a monologue about why she had to get home to Bel-Air, which she loved so much. Emily-as-Spazmo was supposed to tell her why Bel-Air was lame and why everything was better in the mountains, where you could be alone. In the middle of this, Kimmie was supposed to cry, but Kimmie couldn't fake tears on command, so she turned her head away from the audience and buried her face in her shoulder.

Knowing that Kimmie would be turning away from the audience, Emily waited until that exact moment to cry real tears, which she could fake on command. "It's better to be alone!" she yelled, letting the tears stream down her face. As they trickled along her cheeks, the audience became so quiet and still, she could hear people breathing. They were listening to every word she said.

Emily had the strange feeling that the audience was *on her side*. It was as though everything that came out of her mouth was funny when it was supposed to be funny, even when she was just reacting to Kimmie (who wasn't getting any of the laughs). And when she was serious and sad, it felt like the audience actually *cared.*

By the time she had to do her monologue, Emily knew the audience was enjoying the show. And she felt proud that she'd elevated a mediocre script into something that was watchable. She walked to the center of the stage, the lights warm on her head, to begin her monologue. "You're a judger or you're a hater. But guess what? So am I! I judged my hometown and I hated it. I judged myself and I hated that. And I came to the mountains. And I'm still that girl I'm running away from! You can run away, but you can't hide from yourself!"

Emily delivered her last line. "Don't be like me, living alone in the mountains, judging and hating, waiting until the day a girl rings your doorbell and gives you something else to judge and hate. Go live in Bel-Air and meet people and hear their stories and love the life you've been given!" The red curtains fell and slowly slid together, blocking the audience from Emily's sight.

And then, just when the edges of the curtains kissed, Emily breathed a huge sigh of relief. She was done! It was farewell to Spazmo and *Judgers & Haters* forever. And she had already clicked into another role: Networking Actress.

Emily didn't want to waste any time before meeting Hank Myler and giving him the chance to realize that she was perfect for his upcoming film *If You Say So*. Still in her headgear and plaid woodsman-y flannel, she darted out the stage door into the courtyard, where the audience waited for cast members.

"Good job!" Becks said, hugging Emily. "I needed a good laugh after today." Emily smiled gratefully: She knew Becks's heart had been broken just a few hours ago, and she was so touched that Becks was there to support her. "Mac went to *el baño*. Too many Red Bulls," Becks added.

"Mac's not here?" Emily squeaked nervously. Emily glanced at the line for the bathroom, which was several girls long. She glanced at Kimmie, who was so close to Hank Myler. She couldn't risk waiting for Mac and losing her shot at talking to Hank. She groaned inwardly, realizing she'd have to brave this without Mac's guidance.

"She said good job and she'll be out here in five," Becks said easily, missing how *crew-shal* it was for Emily to have Mac around. Especially right now.

Kimmie was standing a few feet away, hugging her grandparents. "How sweet that you wrote a play for such a troubled classmate!" her grandmother cooed. Emily smiled, secretly pleased that she'd fooled even strangers with her performance. She truly was an actress.

Becks leaned in, as if to hug Emily, and then she grabbed her shoulders and whispered right into her ear, "Don't look now, but Hank Myler is walking *righttowardyou*."

Emily slowly tried to take off her headgear, since it made speaking difficult. She needed to be as different as possible from Spazmo when she met Hank Myler so that he would be impressed with her range.

"You didn't tell me you went to school with the next Cate Blanchett! What chops that girl has," Hank exclaimed to his daughter, who was standing next to him near a corner of the courtyard. They were just a few feet away from Becks and Emily. "Let's go say hi!"

Emily's heart soared.

"No, Daddy, she's not my friend," Minka Myler protested.

Emily froze. Becks stared at her, concerned.

"What do you mean?" Hank said. "She's comedy gold."

Minka leaned into her father and whispered, "She's *really* Spazmo. She wasn't acting." Emily thought back to the time she'd winked at Minka in Spanish class. They hadn't been sharing a moment. All this time, Minka had thought she had issues!

Emily wanted to go talk to Hank but she couldn't get her headgear off. She spun around frantically, remembering Mac's words to her on the first day of school: *People believe whatever you tell them*. She desperately had to do her own PR. She yanked at her headgear in one panicky attempt to shake herself from its grip.

When she looked up, she realized: Hank Myler was staring at her sadly. The way he was looking at her reminded Emily of how she had felt when she read about a two-headed snake in Spain: just amazed and creeped out that it actually existed. Emily wished she could slither away.

She knew that if Hank Myler had a *conversation* with her, and saw how *surprisingly not-Spazmo* she was, he'd be once again impressed with her "chops." She yanked the headgear off her face, forgetting that it was clasped behind her head, too. Frantic to look normal before she lost her window of opportunity, she waved at Hank with her left hand while she fiddled with her headgear with her right hand.

Hank held up his hand, almost like he was saying, *Stop.*

First impressions are everything—Emily could hear Mac's first-day-of-school warning. Between the greeting and the one-handed headgear removal, Emily realized she'd gone too far down the freak-show path.

"Hey, where's your friend Kimmie?" Hank leaned over to Minka. They seemed to have no idea their voices carried in the closed courtyard. Emily's eyed widened like a mother bear's realizing someone was after her cub. *That role was hers!* She put both hands to her headgear and snapped it off. And then, Hulk Hogan style, she ripped off her flannel clothes, dressing down to her Rock & Republic jeans and James Perse tee. When she looked up to chase after the Mylers, she realized it was too late: Hank was already shaking hands with Kimmie.

"So I'm working on this film called *If You Say So,*" Hank was saying, but Emily couldn't bear to listen to the rest. She turned around and buried her head in Becks's shoulder, knowing she was never going to work in this town again.

CHAPTER TWENTY-SEVEN

mac

◀ Saturday September 19 ▶

8:45 PM ExtravaBAMSa finale

9:02 PM TDR! Take Down Ruby!

10:30 PM I.C. slumber party (whewsies! We need a party after this week!)

ExtravaBAMSa could not end soon enough, Mac decided, as she popped a portobello mushroom quesadilla into her mouth. Standing by the buffet table, she surveyed the Tachman Center, the formal room used only for super-red-carpet events. The ExtravBAMSa closing ceremonies always featured a catered dinner and a speech by the newly elected social chair.

It was bad enough that Mac had to wear her Loomstate organic gingham dress to a formal affair, thanks to Ruby's no-dupes rules. The dress was the only not-yet-debuted piece in her closet. But because it was so casual and unassuming looking, no one would ask about it. And no one would know that it was 100 percent cotton, grown free of pesticides, or that it had been designed by Bono's wife. So Mac just looked plain for no reason, and got no props for her environmentally friendly choices. And on top of *that*, she knew she would have to witness

Ruby being the star. Ugh. It was enough to make her want to barf all over her organic dress.

That night the Tachman Center, which had wall-to-wall windows overlooking Benedict Canyon, had been decorated with hundreds of circular tables, covered in white tablecloths, with white tulips in the center. The walls were plastered with maps of Africa and SAVE DARFUR banners. Photographs of Sudan, donated to the event by *National Geographic,* hung from the ceiling, and a slide show about Africa played on the back wall. A musical group, flown in from Darfur, played drums while the crowd mingled.

Mac bitterly surveyed the scene: It was classy, international, and appropriate.

Because Mac had secretly approved every choice.

Mac had considered not going to the finale, but then decided she'd just look bitter, like when Leonardo DiCaprio skipped the Oscars when he got snubbed for a nomination. Of course, Mac *was* bitter. She just didn't want to show it. But thankfully, it would be over soon.

Mac scoured the crowd, spotting her mother and father, who were mingling with Kimmie's parents, Elliot and Tina Tachman, who had long blond hair that was clearly courtesy of extensions. They were laughing so loud that Mac could hear them from across the room. Clutch Becks and his buddies from his TV show *That Was Clutch* were at another table. Even Barry Goldman, wearing Ray-Ban sunglasses despite the fact that it was (a) indoors and (b) nighttime, made a cameo.

Mac stood with her best friends by the food tables. They looked sadder than movie stars who'd overdosed on plastic surgery. Becks was twirling a Sprinkles dark chocolate cupcake in one hand, sticking her tongue out to lick off the icing. Coco sipped a strawberry mocktail, stirring her tall glass sadly. Emily stood next to them holding her stomach with one arm and chewing on a strand of her long cinnamon-brown hair. Mac never encouraged her friends to look too happy at parties, but looking this sad was even worse.

Mac clapped her hands, calling them to attention. "Girls, don't worry. I've got it all under control." Even though the rest of the I.C. sabotages hadn't gone quite right, this was the one element of the comeback track that *she* controlled, and Mac had utter faith in her ability to make things happen. She'd run off earlier to make sure her plan was in effect, claiming she'd had one too many Red Bulls.

Coco smiled sadly, like she felt bad for Mac. "What's to control?" She shrugged. "Tonight I became the biggest freak in the history of BAMS."

"At least people here knew you before," Emily whined. "I'm just Spazmo forever."

"Austin haaaaates me," Becks said. A mother in a black velvet dress gently pushed Becks to the side so she could reach for a cupcake.

"Girls, let's have our pity party later, okay?" Mac said, channeling her inner Adrienne. She lowered her voice and the girls moved closer. "When Ruby blows it tonight, there's a very good chance she'll be overthrown as social chair. And this whole regime will crumble. Your life can change like *that*." Mac snapped her fingers.

Coco stared at Mac like she had suddenly turned into an African elephant. "Why would Ruby blow anything? She's been really, really good at ruining our lives."

"I'd say she's a world-class expert," Becks chimed in.

Emily smiled encouragingly at Mac, trusting her scheming.

Mac shrugged impishly. "You just never know. I would just feel so bad for her if the song she is about to lip-synch was swapped with say, some really mortifying lyrics about how she hates BAMS, is half gorilla, and secretly loves the Shean twins."

"Are you nuts?" Coco hissed, awestruck. Becks and Emily looked at each and then looked back at their alpha friend.

Mac was staring intently at the podium. She spoke in a toneless voice. "Let's just say that I might have encouraged Ruby to record and lip-synch her song, and let's just say that maybe what I gave the dude in the sound booth was"—Mac made air quotes—"*accidentally* the wrong CD."

"Are you for serious?" Coco smiled mischievously.

"That's why you're my hero," Emily said proudly.

"For reals." Becks nodded.

"Ladies and gentlemen," Headmaster Billingsley's voice boomed. "How about a big hand for the young lady who made this all possible? Miss Ruby Goldman!"

Mac shot a glance over to the other side of the room, where Ruby stood flanked by the Rubybots, who beamed as though their names had been called. Ruby was wearing a pink Calypso sundress and silver Charlotte Ronson sandals. Ellie was wearing a teal Elijah one-shoulder minidress, looking slightly slutacious, and Haylie wore a pantsuit. Kimmie, who had changed into a pink Juicy Couture sundress, was sitting by her computer studiously, live-blogging the event for the BAMS intranet.

"Isn't that your Calypso dress?" Coco asked Mac, eyeing Ruby's ensemble.

"Apparently Ruby and I have the same taste." Mac shrugged. "And by 'the same' I mean *mine*."

Ruby hobbled to the front of the auditorium on her shiny crutches while the crowd watched silently, reverently. Mac surveyed the room, recognizing almost all the parents. Across the sea of tablecloths and tulips, she spotted her mother and father clapping politely and winced, wishing they were clapping for *her* social chair speech. "Get ready for Gettysburg." Mac rolled her eyes. She did not want to have to see Ruby give the speech that should have been hers. *Was this how Hilary Duff felt when she saw Joel and Nicole?*

Ruby made her way up the stage and took her place

behind the podium. The room became quiet and the Inner Circle leaned in nervously, waiting for signs that Mac's work had kicked in. "First of all, I would like to sing a song that I have written for BAMS. It's a single from my upcoming album, to be released by BP Records this spring."

There were some oohs and aaahs from the crowd.

Mac held her breath. She couldn't wait for Ruby to fake-sing her song, and then have something embarrassing come out instead. It would be a cross between the Ashlee Simpson *SNL* tragedy and Mac's own Slumbergate disaster—but on an even larger scale. Mac was filled with nervous energy, like when she watched Olympic gymnasts on the balance beam, waiting for them to fall.

Ruby's voice crooned perfectly over the speakers.

Wham BAMS
Thank you, ma'am
You made me who I am
You taught me what I know

Nothing about half gorillas, nothing about love for the Shean twins. What was worse—Ruby looked like she was having fun. She was really owning her performance, covering the stage, making eye contact all over the room, singing loud and proud. Mac checked the room for signs of nausea or disgust, but no one was smirking. Parents (even hers!) were smiling. A bald man at the table behind her parents was snapping to the beat, like a guest at an expensive, classy sing-along. Mac rolled her eyes.

You made me who I am
You taught me what I know

When Ruby finished, the crowd applauded wildly. Mac felt sick.

Ruby beamed proudly. Then she bowed with her head like she was in yoga class saying *Namaste.* She walked to the podium and leaned close to the microphone. "I would like to thank all of you for being here tonight to support our great institution and the cause of saving Darfur." If she was nervous about speaking in front of such a big crowd, she didn't show it. "Though I must give credit where credit is due. I couldn't have put this event together without the help of my assistant, Mac Little-Fartstrong. . . ."

There were tiny giggles, mostly from BAMS students. Mac stared straight ahead at the stage, refusing even to blink. She absolutely would not show how embarrassed she was by such a stupid joke or the fact that she had been outed as an assistant in front of all the families.

Ruby cleared her throat. "Armstrong. Excuse me. Her generous help in ways big and small—very, *very* small—has made this event the success it was."

The Inner Circle exchanged uncomfortable glances.

Mac pursed her Chanel-coated lips together and searched the room to see her mother's reaction. At that exact second, Adrienne turned to face Mac and their eyes locked. But Mac couldn't tell what Adrienne was thinking—she had a natural poker face. She went back to listening intently to Ruby's speech, leaving Mac feeling even more embarrassed. Her mother would *never* allow herself to be humiliated in front of a group of people. *How could she have played this so badly?*

"Thank you all so much for being here." Ruby smiled demurely. The crowd applauded politely and Ruby daintily hobbled off the stage.

Mac was fuming inside. She stared at her friends. They were in shock, like war victims. Not only had Ruby publicly humiliated Mac yet again, she'd managed to look humble and well spoken in the process. It was like throwing salt on their wounds and then wounding them again.

Ruby hobbled all the way back to the buffet, where the Inner Circle was standing. "Nice try, Macdaddy," Ruby hissed through her fake smile. "I really did trust you and then you tried to blast me. Don't worry—it'll never happen again." Then she went back to join the Rubybots, who were clapping excitedly, like Ruby had just won an Oscar.

Mac swallowed and realized she was experiencing a

very uncomfortable sensation. It was the feeling of not getting what she wanted. *Was this how other people felt all the time?* Mac shook herself to ease the tension. All the AmExes and dues-paying in the world couldn't buy back her reputation now.

CHAPTER TWENTY-EIGHT

becks

◄ Sunday September 20 ►

7:45 AM Wake up and surf

11 AM Wake my friends up

12 PM Go back to surfing

Becks's eyes were puffy when she woke up in her screening room the morning after ExtravaBAMSa to the sound of crashing waves and a barking dog. She checked her G-Shock watch: It was only 7:45 a.m.

She wiped the sleep from her eyes and remembered why she felt so exhausted: On the Sad Scale of 1 to 10, the Inner Circle sleepover had been a 200, culminating in a double feature of *The Notebook* and *Steel Magnolias*. They'd spent the whole night crying until they finally fell asleep.

Becks woke up while her friends were fast asleep in her screening room. Mac's mouth was hanging wide open, her arm draped over her American Apparel track shorts. Coco, in Victoria's Secret Pink pajamas, was snoring every third breath. Emily was curled in a ball on the couch, wearing her Harajuku Lovers pajama set.

Knowing she'd never be able to fall back asleep, Becks decided to sneak out to catch some surf. It was the only thing that could make her feel almost normal again. At that moment, she just felt like a tall, mean person with really jittery nerves.

She grabbed a Daisy May longboard from her rack and slipped out to the beach, breathing the salty, windy air. It was such a clear day that in the distance she could see the cliffs of Palos Verdes Peninsula and its red-tiled houses. Down the sand, Ellen Pompeo, Becks's neighbor, was splashing her feet in the water. She gave Becks a cute wave as she headed down the beach. Becks waved back and inhaled the coconut sunscreen and saltwater scent that was Malibu.

Becks had barely stepped onto the sand when she spotted a familiar red and black plaid blanket and a goldendoodle. Down the beach about fifty yards, Austin was tossing a red Frisbee to his dog, Boone.

Becks paused at the end of her backyard. Austin Holloway was at the top of the list of People Becks Did Not Want to See. She could forge ahead to the beach, hold her head up high, and pretend like nothing had happened, or she could sneak back into her house and avoid another uncomfortable moment with Austin. He knew too many embarrassing things about her: the Pinkberry Slobber, sabotaging Ellie, the fact that she'd even had a crush on him in the first place—there was only so much humiliation a girl could handle. She was tired of strategizing ways to win his heart.

And then Becks realized: No matter how hard you

tried, you couldn't make someone like you. All the scheming, hoping, wishing, conniving—no boy was worth that much energy. And it didn't work anyway. Becks was too sad to care.

She tiptoed back into the house and into the kitchen. Her father was at the emerald green granite countertop, holding down the top to the blender while a pink concoction whizzed inside. He was off the total body cleanse but not yet on solid foods. Becks waited until the whirr had subsided. Spotting Becks, he smiled.

"Hey, you! What a day yesterday, huh?" he said, as he poured the strawberry-banana concoction into a tall clear glass. "How's your friend Ellie? She took quite a spill."

Becks looked down at the slate floor in shame, actually feeling worse than she had just seconds ago.

"She's fine," Becks said, hoping to end all Ellie talk.

"What a trooper," Clutch said. Becks rolled her eyes that yet one more person in her world thought Ellie was great.

"You okay, Evie?" Clutch asked, looking at his daughter in concern. He only called her by that nickname when he was serious, which wasn't very often.

"Hey, Pops, do you think you could drive me to Zuma today? I'd like some new scenery," Becks said, twirling her Inner Circle ring at the end of a short silver chain.

"What's wrong with our scenery?" Clutch asked,

looking out the sliding glass screen door and staring at the stretch of empty white sand. Becks followed his gaze and caught a glimpse of Austin waxing his board.

"Everything," Becks sighed.

She'd finally accepted it: No matter how well she surfed, she couldn't surf her way into Austin's heart. Evangelina Becks, the girl who never quit, had officially given up.

CHAPTER TWENTY-NINE

COCO

◀ Sunday September 20 ▶

11:30 AM Is it bad to go home and sleep some more?

1 PM In-house spa therapy—paraffin mani? I need some ME-HAB!

Coco got a ride back to the King Bel-Air Hotel from Erin and Mac and lazily dragged her knee-high Uggs (which, for the record, she only wore to slumber parties or when the temperature was below 70 degrees) into the Living Quarter. The first thing she saw when she opened the front door was her mother, sitting on the couch. Cardammon was sipping what looked like a mimosa, and petting Coco's French bulldog, Madonna, who was curled in her lap, wearing a black dog tee that said RUFF. They were bathed in sunlight pouring through the French doors.

Coco looked at her mom with her tired eyes. Even though it was Sunday, Cardammon was wearing a black satin tube dress with a zipper down the middle. She was surrounded by tiered trays of mini scones and thin sandwiches, like she was having a tea party all by herself.

"Are you okay?" Coco asked, wondering what in the world this was about. She already felt bad enough about embarrassing her family at ExtravaBAMSa—she didn't need any more surprises.

Cardammon raised her champagne flute. "It's for you! We're celebrating!" Madonna yelped from Cardammon's lap.

"Celebrating what?"

"You're dee-lish just the way you are," Cardammon declared, sounding very much like she'd rehearsed every word with her life coach, Dee Dufflin.

Coco smiled weakly. "This is really lovely, Mom." She sized up the cucumber sandwiches and the porcelain teacups and mini Bonne Maman jams. Coco knew her mother was only trying to comfort her after weeks of seeing her dreams get crushed. Sure, it was terrible to have been rejected by the world's most famous record producer (three weeks ago). Of course it was awful to have been demoted from dance captain (almost two weeks ago). And yes, ExtravaBAMSa had been beyond humiliating (last night). But Coco didn't regret any of it. The way she saw it, September had been a really bad month. And surely there were better things on the horizon. As the light sparkled off Cardammon's pebble-size yellow diamond ring, Coco realized: She hadn't gone through any of that to please her mother. She'd done it for herself.

"I've pushed you far too hard with the dancing and the pop star thing," Cardammon said in a serious tone. "I wanted you to have this life because I've enjoyed it, but no one *needs* this." Cardammon waved at a row of her own framed platinum records on the wall. "Seeing those every morning isn't what makes me happy."

"I was born to perform," Coco said, believing it, but wondering why she felt so defensive. "I do this because there's nothing I love more."

Cardammon looked down at the pale green carpet, her expression like a sad Norah Jones song.

Was her own mother telling her she should quit?

Coco bit her lip and thought of her idol, Christina Aguilera. Xtina didn't give up. Xtina had gone before the whole world in trashy, stomach-baring outfits with black makeup and fake braids before she glammed it up, went multiplatinum (hair and records), got married, and had a baby, Coco reminded herself, twirling her Inner Circle ring. But then again . . . Xtina had been the most talented girl in America by age six. No one thought Coco had that kind of talent. In fact, everyone thought Coco was embarrassingly bad.

Especially Coco.

She let go of the ring. Maybe it was just easier to give in. Why fight it? Even her own mother was holding open the escape hatch.

Coco smiled and reached for a pumpkin scone, lathering it with thick whipped cream from a white ceramic pot, even though she didn't much feel like eating. Normally she only ate when she was hungry, but now she just wanted to take her mind off dancing.

"Cheers, Mom," Coco said, numbly raising her scone to her mother's glass. She was tired of fighting—for her place on the team, for dancing, for her reputation, for approval. It was so much easier to just go with the flow.

"Cheers, luvvy," Cardammon said. She tapped her glass against Coco's scone.

It was time to take a bite out of reality, Coco decided. It was time to stop living in a pop star dream world. As she bit into the still-warm scone, she realized it didn't even taste good. In fact, much like reality, it was very unappetizing.

CHAPTER THIRTY

emily

◀ Sunday September 20 ▶

12 PM CALL MOM

Emily stared up at the ecru-colored wall of the guest bedroom, her home for the last two weeks. The Armstrongs called the guest bedroom the Gift Closet, because it was where they kept all the presents they didn't want to throw away but didn't want to keep on display. Emily's eyes landed on a heart-shaped jewelry box, a gift to Adrienne from Ben Affleck and Jennifer Garner. Then she shifted her gaze to the signed *Shakespeare in Love* poster (from Gwyneth Paltrow) and the Princess Diana commemorative plate (from Elton John) and the brass owl (from Owen Wilson).

On better days, Emily had found the gifts cool. But today, everything about the Gift Closet felt uncomfortable, and not at all like home. It was just a stark reminder that she wasn't in Iowa anymore, where her walls were covered in yellowed pictures of Davey Woodward ripped from magazines, and goofy self-portraits of her and Paige at Winky's Donuts.

Through her windows overlooking the Armstrongs' swimming pool, Emily spied Mac lying in the hammock, lazily flipping through a French *Vogue* under the shade of a palm frond—which she knew was Mac's go-to de-stress activity. Mac's brother, Jenner, was practicing his volleyball serve on the lawn by the pool, and Mac's fluffy-haired little sister, Maude, was playing at her laptop computer. Jenner walked over to the pool and scooped out a handful of water to throw at Mac. She jerked back and shot him a disgusted look. Maude giggled from behind her computer. Even teasing each other, they looked like such a family. It made Emily feel like more of an outsider. It wasn't her family. It wasn't her home.

She picked up the cordless phone from the silver side table and dialed her mom's number. She wished she could click her heels three times and magically be back in Iowa.

Lori Mungler picked up on the first ring. "Hey, hunny, how's it going?" She took a bite of what sounded like a Cheeto. The TV was on in the background, and Emily could hear *Dr. Phil*, which her mom must have TiVo'd, because his show wasn't on on Sundays.

Emily felt a tear trickle down her cheek as she listened to the sounds of home. She couldn't believe that she was getting wistful thinking about Cheetos and Dr. Phil, and *that* thought only made her more sad. Normally Emily could control her tears, but these days, it seemed like all she did was cry uncontrollably.

"Sweetheart . . ." Lori paused to swallow. She lowered the volume on the TV. "Is everything okay with Mac and the girls?"

"Yesbutitsnotworkingformeasanactress!" Emily cried, her chest heaving up and down. She stared at the brass owl. Its carved eyes looked like they were judging her. Even the brass owl thought she was a loser.

"Sweetie, take deep breaths, okay? Everything in life happens for a reason. I miss you, too. But remember, you don't have these opportunities in Iowa."

"I know, I don't care!" Emily cried. Tears streamed down her face. "I want to be home."

"Sweetheart, it'll all be okay. When you know what you want, then you can put it into the universe." Lori soothed. Normally Emily rolled her eyes at her mother's *Secret*-inspired wisdom, but today its familiarity filled her with relief. Emily was quiet and her breathing slowed.

Finally, when she was able to speak coherently once again, she said, very calmly, so her mother would know she was being serious: "This was a huge mistake and I hate Bel-Air."

There was a rattle at the door. Emily looked up and saw Mac standing in the doorway, holding a glass pitcher full of lemonade. Mac clutched it with both hands, her eyes wide open like she'd seen a ghost. The look on Mac's face gave it away: She'd heard everything. She turned and left.

"Oh no," Emily gasped.

"Ems, are you still there?" Lori asked.

Emily looked at the phone and then the empty doorway, feeling even more powerless than she had ten seconds ago. Nothing she put into the universe was any good.

CHAPTER THIRTY-ONE

mac

◀ Sunday September 20 ▶

ALL DAY SORRY EVERYONE. Please don't drink the haterade, 'cause I'm working on it

Mac tiptoed as quickly as she could down the stairway from Emily's room, holding tight to the banister. She felt her life spinning out of control. She'd failed as an agent and as a friend. She'd lost social chair, her reputation had tanked, and now, her only client (who happened to be her good friend) was ditching her.

Mac needed to talk to her mother—who, as usual, was working on a sunny Sunday afternoon. Adrienne was in her home office, on the phone, raking her Japanese rock garden, when she looked up and spotted Mac. She held up her index finger to show that she'd be right with her.

"All righty, Milo, I'll get into this some more tomorrow. You be a good boy in Vegas," she said. "No pictures in *Us Weekly*, okay? Promise?" After a pause, once Milo had clearly hung up the phone, Adrienne leaned into her hands-free headset to speak to her assistant, who had also been listening in on the call. "Are we clear, Charlotte?" Adrienne asked.

Mac couldn't believe that her mother's office assistants got paid to eavesdrop on phone calls and take notes on what celebrities said. Or that her mother was so powerful that some poor assistant actually had to work on a Sunday, dialing phone numbers and connecting Adrienne to A-list clients so that she didn't have to do it herself.

"Thanks for the good work, Charlotte. Especially on a Sunday. We're done for today. You can come in at nine tomorrow." Adrienne flicked off her headset and looked at Mac, who had slunk into the Eames chair across from her desk.

"Brighten up," Adrienne said perkily.

Mac doubled-checked that her mother was not still on the phone. Sometimes she was talking to other people and Mac didn't realize it.

Negative. The headset was definitely on the table.

"How can I brighten up when I'm a big failure?" Mac asked. She looked at her mother's framed black-and-white pictures of 1920s Los Angeles Art Deco buildings. "I mean, you were at the fund-raiser—you saw what happened."

Mac looked down at her red Toms shoes, not wanting to hear her mother rub it in. "Mackenzie, I'm so proud of you," Adrienne said. Mac looked up at her mother, sure she hadn't heard right. "Emily showed everyone what a talented actress she is," Adrienne continued, as if reading Mac's mind. "I'll bet the only reason she didn't quit that dreadful play was because *you* encouraged her to make something of that role." Adrienne pushed her Armani glasses against her nose. "Am I right?"

"How did you know that?" Mac's eyed widened. For the first time in a while, she felt a sense of accomplishment: She had made her mother proud, and that was one of the best feelings in the world.

"It's what we do. We push people to make the best choices for themselves," Adrienne sighed. "Tristin may be a fireball of talent," Adrienne said, referring to her two-time Oscar-winning client, "but if it weren't for me, she'd get one-liners on *How I Met Your Mother*."

Mac buzzed with hope for just a second. Maybe things weren't so bad after all? But then she remembered that she'd failed. Emily was leaving for Iowa. And this time, she'd have no reason to believe Mac if she tried to stop her. As if remembering her true loser status, Mac blurted, "But if I've done such a good job, then how come I'm so subprime at BAMS? I did what you said—I paid my dues—and no one will deal with me anymore."

"Did you do your best?" Adrienne asked.

Mac nodded slowly. She'd done it right initially, holding up her end of the deal. But then she remembered the moral detour she had taken when she decided to sabotage the Rubybots. She thought about how that plan had completely backfired, and sunk them even deeper into the self-centered off-ramp of misery. If only she'd stayed on track and followed her mother's advice! Then maybe none of this would have happened.

"Your best is all you can do." Adrienne shrugged as if it were all no big deal. She clasped her hands and leaned toward Mac. "Let me tell you a little story," Adrienne sighed. "Remember that agent who made me go by the name Audrey? Well, I gave it three months. Then, when I realized he wasn't going to promote me, I convinced another partner in the agency to hire me."

Mac gasped. She'd encouraged all her friends to work hard based on false pretenses. "But I thought you said you had to pay your dues?"

"Yes, but you have to be smart about *where* you pay them. And you have to know when to cut your losses. I got off his desk, worked for another partner—the one who wanted all those peanut butter shakes—and within a year I was a junior agent. I even got my own e-mail address."

Mac thought about this. When her mom had hit a wall, she'd switched bosses. But there was no way she could transfer schools two weeks into the year. "But BAMS is the only boss in my world." Mac sighed.

"Who said anything about BAMS?" Adrienne shook her head. "You have to think outside the BAMS box," she continued with a knowing look.

Mac looked at her mom as if she had fallen from the sky. "Mom, you're losing me."

"You did great in Hollywood a few weeks ago," Adrienne said. "You got Emily seen for the hottest project in town. I have agents working for me who *still* can't get their clients in front of Elliot Tachman."

Mad nodded, feeling a tiny bit proud.

"It seems like you've been spending an awful lot of time worrying about the small dogs, and now it's time to pony up for the big dogs." Adrienne winked.

Mac shook her head. *How* did her mother always know the answer to everything?

"Oh, and by the way, tomorrow you should check out *Variety*. I know things have been tough, but you have to stay on top of industry news." With that, Adrienne picked up a script with a red Initiative logo and kicked her heels on her desk, signaling that their conversation was over.

Mac smiled. Of course she would check out *Variety*. She used to read it every day, before she became so wrapped up in Pax Rubana and lost sight of her real goal: Hollywood domination. She and her friends were lucky enough to know exactly what they wanted to do with their lives. Why scale it down to BAMS size?

Mac thought about the girl she'd been for the past seven days. And then, as with the skinny jeans trend, Mac knew:

It was time to say *adieu*!

CHAPTER THIRTY-TWO

emily

◀ Monday September 21 ▶

12 PM Mac, where are you?

When the lunch bell rang, Emily walked very slowly to her locker, dragging her checkerboard Vans so that each step took twice as long as it should have. She felt weighed down by a horrible sense of guilt. It had been so painful to see Mac, always strong, actually vulnerable and sad because of things *she* had said. She must have seemed so ungrateful. Emily wished she could rewind and close the door when she'd been talking to her mom. *How could she have been so stupid?*

She was in no rush to join Becks and Coco at their Z-list table. Not that she had anywhere else to go. Mac was MIA—she hadn't ridden to school with Emily and hadn't been in homeroom—and Emily couldn't shake the feeling that it was all her fault.

As Emily took in BAMS's red-tiled roof, its blazing bougainvillea, and the mystic-tanned kids lounging on the lawn, she felt a little nostalgic for BAMS, knowing she was leaving. She still hadn't told Becks or Coco, and she wasn't sure when she would.

Emily, Becks, and Coco met at the entrance to the food hall, grabbed their trays, and headed to the vegetarian section. They each grabbed an M Café tofu bento box.

"Dude, I haven't seen Mac all day," Becks said, opening her box before they'd even swiped their charge cards. She reached in and grabbed a tofu square, nibbling at the corners.

"She's totally MIA." Coco glanced down at her phone. "Six unanswered texts."

"Do you think Mac is sick?" Emily asked hopefully. It was a better prospect than Mac being so depressed that she had to take a mental health day.

"Who knows?" Becks shrugged.

"This is so unlike her," Coco said somberly, checking her phone one more time.

Emily didn't know what to say. She hadn't even felt this anxious before performing as Spazmo in front of a packed house. Only Mac could give a girl this much anxiety. They walked in silence to their usual table, with no energy to strut.

The girls opened their bento boxes and began pecking at the tofu squares inside. Emily couldn't think of anything new to talk about other than the fact that she was leaving, and she didn't feel like dumping more bad news on Becks and Coco.

After several minutes of non-golden silence, Emily

felt a hand on her shoulder. The scent of Essie wafted under her nose.

Mac!

She was wearing a brand-new Marni sundress with a scoop neck. Her silver Inner Circle ring beamed brightly off its long chain.

"I'm glad to see we're in the mood for sushi," Mac said, eyeing the boxes on the girls' trays. "And I'm glad to see you haven't done too much damage, 'cause I made rezzies."

Becks, Coco, and Emily looked at one another with curious smiles.

"Follow me," Mac said simply.

The girls left their bento boxes on the table and followed Mac out the door and to the front of the BAMS driveway, where Erin was waiting in a black Mercedes S600 sedan.

"Why is Erin driving a new car?" Becks asked.

"Because today is a new day," Mac said. "But the car is only for today."

"Oh no!" Coco groaned. "Have you been spending time with Cardamommy?"

"What's so special about today?" Becks asked.

"Today," Mac said, holding the door open so her friends could crawl into the backseat, "is the first day of the rest of our lives." She closed the door and hopped into the front. "Which is why we are going to celebrate at Katsuya."

Erin whirled around and cheerily faced the group. "You guys, I seriously like don't know how to drive this. OHMYGOSH!" Erin giggled. The Benz was tricked out with a Garmin GPS, DVD player, and the finest leather steering wheel. Erin honked the horn.

"Take it down a notch, GPS," Mac said affectionately, using her nickname for Erin. Emily hadn't heard that nickname for Erin since the night she'd met Mac. And then she realized: With that coy remark, *that* Mac was back. The girl who had chased after her at a party and almost made her a movie star in seventy-two hours. The girl who made the impossible possible.

"Girls, I realized, I've been thinking too small for all of us," Mac said. "We have the whole world at our fingertips." She reached into her purple Mulberry Mabel bag and pulled out a business card, which she waved in the air like a Polaroid picture. "Remember Chad Hutchins?" Mac said, thrusting the card toward Becks. "Becks, my dear, you are going to be Roxy's next great surf talent slash model," she said. "I've already pitched you to him. He can't wait to come see you surf in the 'Bu."

Becks's jaw dropped and she reached for the card. "I figured I blew it. Are you sure?" Becks asked, befuddled.

Mac nodded. "And if you still want Austin, once he sees you on every billboard on Sunset Boulevard, you'll definitely get out of the friend zone. But we're not doing this for *him,* we're doing this for *you.* He's just vegan icing on the dairy-free cupcake." Becks grinned and slid the business card into her jeans pocket.

Mac turned to Coco. "Remember that crazy water boy song of yours that I interrupted? Sure, it was nuts, but you've got an amazing voice, my little chanteuse."

Coco nodded gratefully, her eyes twinkling.

Mac continued. "You've been going down the Britney Spears path and—duh!" Mac tapped her temple, like she was having an "aha" moment. "You're way more Jewel circa '99, minus the whole living-in-a-van thing. Big duh."

Coco beamed as if the clouds had parted and pure, bright sunlight was streaming down onto her pretty head.

Emily watched her friends' moods soar and she stared at Mac in awe. She had never seen anyone inspire people the way Mac did. Or so fearlessly aim for the top. She didn't even mind that Mac didn't have any grandiose plans for her, or that her problems might not even be fixable. She felt like she was back on the winning team, and that was enough.

"Wait, what about Ruby?" Becks asked. "Are we just going to let her off the hook?"

"Well, if a video montage of her talking smack about Kimmie, bossing me around, and throwing a hissy fit will entertain just the four of us, I can't help that, can I?" Mac raised her eyebrows. She pointed at the flat-screen TV that faced her friends.

"Enjoy!" Mac giggled.

The girls leaned in to stare at the screen. Sure enough, there was a short movie of Ruby bossing Mac around.

"You have to send this to everyone at BAMS!" Coco gasped.

Mac shrugged. "Nah. I think we have bigger and better things to worry about."

Coco, Becks, and Emily nodded. Of course: They *did* have bigger and better things to do. Emily was proud of her group. And she was starting to feel like her pre-BAMS self again.

Mac looked over at Emily. "Lastly, my little starlet. Are you ready for another Davey Woodward kiss?"

"Um . . . I'm not sure what you mean?" Emily stammered. The last time she'd kissed Davey Farris Woodward, colossal movie star, it had been for a movie audition. It had been scary and fun, and ultimately everyone who'd seen her kiss him had rejected her for the part. She didn't want to think about getting rejected uh-gain.

"Elliot saw your play. The man's not an idiot. He's now seen you be a convincing dude, a totally believable spaz, and an adorable all-American Midwestern girl. He had to admit you're phenom." She smiled. "Plus, he was sitting next to my mom, and she had a few convincing words."

Emily's right leg began to tremble. She'd come so close to the part in *Deal With It* so many times, and she'd finally accepted that it wasn't hers. As her mother would say, she'd *let it go*. But was Mac saying that she had the part? Or that Elliot knew she was talented? She twirled a strand of hair nervously around her index finger and looked out the winding roads as they passed palm trees and sprawling Beverly Hills mansions.

Before Emily could experience another nanosecond of fearful doubt, Mac flashed her phone in front of Emily's face. It showed a PDF of today's *Variety*. The headline:

TACHMAN "DEALS WITH" CASTING SHUFFLE
EMILY SKYLER TAPPED FOR CAUFIELD'S ROLE

Emily's eyes widened. She didn't have to scream, because the Inner Circle was screaming for her. Erin honked the horn joyfully.

Mac smiled at her friends. "So, girls, are you ready to be major stars?" She reached into her purse and began pouring a bottle of Orangina into plastic flute glasses she'd brought for the occasion.

"Your success is my success!" Mac passed a drink to each of the girls. "To winning together!"

"Together!" the girls cried in unison, raising their glasses through the sunroof.

"Let's just hope this isn't being recorded," Coco said matter-of-factly.

There was silence in the Benz as the girls sat up and

double-checked for open iChat windows. Then they burst into laugher, knowing they were done with all that.

Mac smiled, her hair whipping triumphantly in the breeze from the sunroof. "This is it, girls. We're almost famous!"

acknowledgments

Thanks to the team: Joelle Hobeika, Sara Shandler, and Josh Bank. I'm also very grateful to Kristin Marang, Andrea C. Uva, Lexa Hillyer, Jessica Rothenberg, and Ben Schrank. And a huge thanks to Joanna Schochet, Ruby Boyd, and Abby Stern.

It's their turn to shine

ZOEY DEAN'S STAR POWER

A TALENT NOVEL

Mac is on a mission: to make her girls stars. Mission Hollywood Domination is in motion! But she quickly discovers that a Tinseltown takeover is not as easy as it seems. Coco's got the voice, but when it comes to the stage, can she out-sparkle her über-famous mom? Becks lands a Quiksilver contract, but will she survive the competitive quicksand? And will Emily ever get another star-kiss from her star-crush? Unless Mac gets in the way . . .

TALENT

YOU EITHER HAVE IT OR YOU DON'T